Mirror Lake

Mirror Lake

Thomas Christopher Greene

CENTURY · LONDON

Published by Century in 2003

1 3 5 7 9 10 8 6 4 2

Copyright © 2003 by Thomas Christopher Greene

Thomas Christopher Greene has asserted his right under the Copyright, Designs and
Patents Act, 1988 to be identified as the author of this work

First published in the United States of America in 2003 by Simon & Schuster, Inc.

First published in the United Kingdom in 2003 by Century

Random House Group Limited
20 Vauxhall Bridge Road, London SW1V 2SA

Random House Australia (Pty) Limited
20 Alfred Street, Milsons Point, Sydney,
New South Wales 2061, Australia

Random House New Zealand Limited
18 Poland Road, Glenfield
Auckland 10, New Zealand

Random House (Pty) Limited
Endulini, 5a Jubilee Road, Parktown 2193, South Africa

Random House Group Limited Reg. No. 954009

www.randomhouse.co.uk

A CIP catalogue record for this book is available
from the British Library

Papers used by Random House
are natural, recyclable products made from wood grown in
sustainable forests. The manufacturing processes conform to
the environmental regulations of the country of origin

ISBN 1 844 13001 0

Typeset by Palimpsest Book Production Limited,
Polmont, Stirlingshire
Printed and bound in Great Britain by
Mackays of Chatham plc,
Chatham, Kent

Author's Note

I began *Mirror Lake* in a café in Northampton, Massachusetts, on a warm summer morning. I finished it a year later in an apartment in Montpelier, Vermont, at two in the morning. In between I wrote in coffeehouses in Montpelier, at friends' houses in the Adirondacks, and often at the picnic table on the side of my house. While the physical writing of it was a solitary act, the larger work that went into the book was not.

Without the support and help of many people, this novel would not have been possible. With gratitude and a measure of humility I want to thank the following: first, my agent, Nick Ellison, whose support and talent have been invaluable in making this book a reality; his assistant, Jennifer Joel, who pulled my work out of a pile of manuscripts and recognized something worth reading; Michael Korda, my editor, for his

Thomas Christopher Greene

his insightful reading, ideas, and editorial work; Bret Lott for
his mentorship; members of the Main Street Writing Group,
Richard Waite, Suzi Wizowati, Judy Fitch, Mary Wells, and
Wilson Ring; Lisa Levangie for first bringing me to Vermont,
helping me find Mirror Lake; my six brothers and sisters for
their belief and encouragement; and, of course, my parents, to
whom this novel is dedicated, for surrounding me with language
and stories and books. Finally, I want to thank Tia McCarthy
for her love, her friendship, and her wisdom.

I should also say that, though I have chosen to set this novel
in Eden, Vermont, it is not meant to represent the actual geography
of that actual northern town. Rather, my Eden is a
composite of places in this state that I know, landmarks that I
love, and places that I have created out of whole cloth.

Thomas Christopher Greene
Montpelier, Vermont
July 21, 2002

vi

FOR MY PARENTS

All roads lead to death.

DON DE LILLO, *White Noise*

Well, I curl into an avalanche,
And I tumble between
Rocks and trees,
I tumble,
Into your wiry arms.

THE BUTTERFLIES OF LOVE,
Love May Be Possible

1

My name is Nathan Carter. Let me say that even though this story does not concern me – not directly, anyway – I feel an obligation to tell it, because it was told to me, and it is the type of story that needs to be told to others, especially now that all the principals are dead. Sometimes in life, as we all know, our experiences collide with another person's in a manner that can only be considered fate: something larger than happenstance, an intermingling of otherwise disparate lives, for a greater purpose. Such was the case, I believe, with my connection to Wallace Fiske, a man whose world should never, under normal circumstances, have come into touch with my own; a man from a different era, from an era that no longer exists in America, except in the small corners and margins of rural life.

It was the summer of 1996, and I had had several seemingly unrelated cathartic experiences in a row, the most notable of which, the death of my father by an untimely heart attack, sent me reeling and scrambling out of Boston, where I had lived for the ten years since I left college; sent me north to the green mountains and valleys of northern Vermont. In Boston, I had been an itinerant student and waiter, someone who, in the language of my class, never seemed to get his act together. I was also a serial monogamist, staying in a relationship with a woman for six months to a year, and then abruptly leaving her; meeting another woman and falling madly, crazily in love, only to beg off as soon as the honeymoon ended.

You could say I had a problem with commitment, and perhaps even intimacy, the kind of intimacy that comes from a love that grows and changes with time; but the truth for me was more complex than any armchair psychology could pin down so neatly. I was at the time, and in truth still am today, a man who tries to anchor himself in the arms of a woman; a man of many fears, most of them irrational; a man afflicted with a syndrome particular to people who shirk the art of living purposefully, focusing all their energy instead on things they can never solve or understand, things like the sky and the spinning of the planet. My cure for this syndrome was fleeting, incandescent love, the kind of love where you never want to get out of bed, where you roll together under cotton sheets, where she enters your thoughts before you fall asleep and is still there when you wake.

I tell you this not simply to illuminate certain truths about me, although it serves that purpose as well, but rather to explain how I came to be so receptive to Wallace Fiske's story, even though I believe that you, as I did, will find his behavior and actions reprehensible.

I AM from a family that traces its roots back to the Pilgrims, and though vast branches are considerably wealthy, with mansions in Chestnut Hill and seaside cottages in Marblehead, somewhere along the line my father's life diverged from those of his Brahmin siblings and I grew up in relatively humble, middle-class neighborhoods around Boston. My father, until his death, sold shoes, though not in a store on his knees with a shoehorn in his hand. He sold wholesale for various companies and made a decent enough living, though he never saved anything and he never told me exactly why he had no claim to the family fortune, other than to show his bitterness sometimes when he had been drinking by pulling out a tattered green copy of the Social Register to show me the names and addresses of all the Carters in it, pointing out the exclusive locations where they lived, the stars next to their names that marked an entirely other level of prestige whose meaning I no longer recall.

Of Mother, for her part, I have only vague memories, since she died when I was six. I do remember a tall, dark-haired woman with a soft voice and a sad face, with deep brown eyes that made her look as if she were perpetually weeping. The last years of her life she spent primarily in bed, dying from a virulent form of bone cancer, and while it affected my life insofar as I grew up motherless, it affected my father much more, for she was his sun and his moon, and after she died he removed all evidence of her from our small ranch house, as if she never existed.

Since my father was always working, and my mother was dead, I spent much of my childhood and adolescence alone, and I learned, in turn, how to take care of myself. I went to school, made friends, and in retrospect was a normal, if shy, boy. Upon high school graduation, I even went to college, not something I was pushed to do but something I thought I should do and, without knowing what it was I wanted out of my future, I studied philosophy, which was a mistake, since it only taught me to move deeper into myself, something I did not need. Nevertheless, I was a competent, if unspectacular, student and managed to graduate in four years, at which point I began waiting tables at Boston restaurants and dating that city's daughters, a pattern I maintained until my father's death.

And so it was that in the summer of 1996, with all the recumbent guilt that comes with losing a parent, I broke it off with yet another girlfriend – this time a tall, skinny divinity school student named Jill – and without much of a plan, but armed with a ten-thousand-dollar inheritance, I packed my spare belongings into my Volkswagen and drove north from Boston to Vermont.

I do not know what I hoped to find amid those green hills in midsummer. I suppose I hoped that instead of anchoring myself in the arms of a woman, and instead of floating ethereally in a world of graduate classes and serving dinner to Bostonians, I would somehow find in that dramatic landscape a way to ground myself in something honest and true;

something that would allow me to get outside myself and my solipsism.

I spent the first days in an Econo Lodge on the fringe of Montpelier, but by the end of the week I had found a rental house in the town of Eden. The house was in reality more of a cabin, a poorly built cabin at that. The landlord, a gruff, hard-drinking New York firefighter, someday wanted to retire here but in the meantime rented it out for five hundred bucks a month. He had built it himself, but from scrap wood, he said, and it was a square structure, with a small porch on the front and two giant windows on the second floor – storefront windows, salvaged when a local department store was razed – so that if you were to look at it head-on the cabin resembled a large, benevolent face. Inside was a small kitchen, a living room beyond that with a woodstove, and then a wooden ladder that led to the upstairs loft, little more than a large, airy room with the storefront windows on the south side.

The cabin was built into the side of the hill, and from the porch and from the storefront windows you could see clear across the valleys of Eden, to the mountains in the distance, the curved horn of Camels Hump interrupting the horizon at sunset. The land around the house was rocky and soon gave way on all sides to a thick forest of poplars, shadbosh, maples, and evergreens. As the house was set down from the dirt road that ran along the ridge of the hill, you could see no other houses from it and, though solitude of this kind seemed the wrong cure for my fears, it struck me as perfect for my needs: out of the way, real, firmly in and of this earth.

Those first months were a matter of adjustment, but I

5

surprised myself by giving in to the rhythms of the place, waking with the sun, sleeping in a bed next to the storefront windows, underneath a canopy of stars in clear weather. During the days I explored the town. First by car, driving around the endless dirt roads that dip and weave through those pitched valleys. I drove by old farmhouses, cows in pastures, pebbly mountain streams with thin waterfalls falling next to the road, run-down trailers tucked into the woods, abandoned cars stacked like pancakes next to them. I drove by old churches with old graveyards, the stones illegible with age. I drove by logging roads cut like seams into the forest, men with heavy equipment dragging the ash and pine down narrow escarpments to muddy clearings, long logs piled high for hauling. I drove by defunct mills, their wheels no longer churning, the clapboards peeling away from the frames. I drove by dirty-faced children playing on the sides of the road. I drove by an old woman wearing hip waders and standing in a child's plastic pool, a slaughtered pig at her feet. I drove by the mix of poor and country wealthy living side by side. I drove each day until I could not drive anymore.

I began to walk. Initially I stuck to the roads, exploring the one I lived on, the surrounding roads. I walked with a big stick to ward off the various dogs that rushed out to meet me. Eventually I grew bolder and began to cut directly into the woods themselves, egging myself on, forcing myself to face the fears of deep forest that anyone who has spent a lifetime in the city has. I walked through meadows of wildflowers, up steeply pitched forest walls, across mountain streams that had slowed to a trickle but that, from the looks of the beds, ran hard and fast with snowmelt in the spring. I walked up the sides of small mountains, above the tree lines, until I could see the undulating hills spread before me, ridges like waves frozen in time.

At night I sat on the porch of that ill-built cabin and watched the gathering dark. I smoked cigarettes and drank scotch and looked at the woods. I looked at the night sky, bright with stars, the moon sometimes sitting crescent-shaped above the mountains. From here I also watched the summer thunder-clouds come over the hills, thick, black clouds, and then the rain in the forest, and then overhead, and then, sitting inside, listened to it pound on the tin roof.

When the fall came and the hills of Eden filled with gold and reds and purples, I decided I needed to find a job. For one thing, I spent all my time alone, and had no friends here, and I needed something to give definition to my days during the winter. I had heard through the owner of the local general store that Mrs Andrews, the woman who delivered the mail for the town, was retiring. Delivering the mail in Eden was unlike delivering mail anywhere else I had been. No uniform, no going door to door with a bag over your shoulder and a can of Mace in one hand. No, it was rural delivery, and they gave you a car, in this case an old Jeep with the steering wheel on the right side.

It took about six hours in good weather to do the job, and this sounded about right to me. It seemed, curiously enough, to fit my circumstances: hardly good work for the college educated, but honest work nonetheless. Good work for a man trying to turn over leaves. I had to take the civil service exam in Montpelier, but I passed it easily, and in the third week of

October 1996, I, Nathan Carter, loosely of the Boston Carters, became the mailman for the town of Eden, Vermont, and this is when Wallace Fiske and I first crossed paths.

THE FISKE house was something of a local landmark. Located at the base of a steep hill that contained what was considered the most dangerous road in Eden, it was one of the oldest in the town, built in the early part of the eighteenth century. Likewise, the Fiske family was one of Eden's oldest and, though they were mostly hill farmers, their land was among the most coveted by the yuppies that had been moving in from Burlington for the past decade. They owned almost three hundred acres, a mixture of woodlands and open pasture, and the house itself was a clapboard cape, and though it was run-down, sinking in places into its foundation, it sat on a small knoll above a crystal blue pond called Mirror Lake that was located entirely on the Fiske land. From that house, as I would discover later, one looked down on the pond and to the hills beyond it and to the line of mountains in the distance.

Wallace Fiske was not a man who received a lot of mail, but if you have an address in America you inevitably get something. His house was one of my last stops, late in the afternoon, when I had been driving those dusty dirt roads for hours, and for weeks I had been putting his mail in the box next to his driveway. I never once saw Wallace during all this time, though I had heard whispering about him in the general store. He was largely regarded, from what I could tell, as one mean bastard, an old man who was best avoided, a man who kept to himself, not even in contact with the many Fiske cousins and relatives that lived in other parts of Eden. What I did see when I dropped off his mail was his dog, a nasty old cur of indeterminate breed that growled at me sideways when I pulled up to the box. I saw his cows, a small herd of Jerseys. Sometimes I also saw his chickens, moving freely across the driveway and into the road.

Then one day, as I was putting his mail in the box – mainly junk flyers from the local Wal-Mart, a catalog of farmer's equipment – I heard someone yelling from out in front of the house, and then around the house came a tall, old man, moving quickly toward the Jeep.

'Get that shit out of here,' he said as he came toward me, and I got my first look at Wallace Fiske. He looked to be in his late seventies, his face heavily lined, his gray hair cut close to his head everywhere except in front, where a sweeping bang came across his forehead. He wore jeans and a brown Carhartt jacket, a pair of work boots. He looked as if he might have been handsome once, almost patrician. He walked fast, though jerkily, as if his knees lacked tendons. He was pissed off.

'Get that shit out of here,' he said again, as he got close.

I leaned out the window. 'Hi,' I said.

'I said, "Get that shit out of here."'

'It's the mail.'

'I don't give a shit what it is. I don't want it here.'

I tried to reason with him. 'It's the mail,' I said again, as if that piece wasn't clear and that, if he understood this much, we could work it out. 'I don't really have a choice. If it has your name on it, I'm supposed to make sure it gets here.'

'Bullshit. You do what you want with it. But don't bring it here.'

And then, before I could say anything else, he had turned on his heels and headed back the way he came, as if everything was settled.

Back at the general store, I told the postmistress, Connie. She chuckled a deep, throaty, cigarette-laced chuckle. 'That's Wallace for you.'

'Well, what do we do?'

'What do you think you do? You keep delivering the mail.'

'Isn't there a form or something he could fill out?'

'For junk mail there is. And that's pretty much all he gets. That and taxes. But he'd have to come in and fill it out. And he won't do that.'

'Can we call him?'

She laughed again. 'Wallace doesn't have a phone.'

'What did Mrs Andrews do?'

'She put up with his shit.'

The following day I was coming down the steep hill before the Fiske house and rounded the bend slowly, looking for him for some reason, as if worried he had set some trap for me, when I noticed that the mailbox itself was gone. I pulled alongside where it had been, and I could see the post hole that was now in the weeds. The dog came out from behind the house and limped toward my car, moving in that odd sideways fashion, its lips sliding over its yellow teeth. It barked twice. There was no sign of Wallace. I looked over his delivery. The local penny saver, another catalog, this one with curtains on the front.

I grabbed the mail and stepped out of the car and began to make my way toward the house. The dog backed up and snarled at me, but I walked right by it. I wasn't worried about the dog. I was taken over by this irrational sense of purpose: I was going to deliver this mail. I didn't have to deliver it. Postal regulations essentially say, 'No box, no mail.' Story over. But delivering the mail was what I did. It was my job, and I liked it. As silly as it sounds, I had bought into the Postal Service creed hook, line, and sinker.

I made it to the door without incident, and I leaned Wallace Fiske's mail neatly against the doorjamb and then headed back to the Jeep. As I drove on, I saw him at the edge of the pond, clearing brush. He stopped as I went by and ran his sleeve across his forehead, but when I waved he went back to work.

We went on like this for months. Once a week I put notices on his door outlining the regulations regarding rural mail-boxes. But I was determined to deliver his mail and I did, even though it meant getting out of the Jeep to do so. If he had wanted to come at me cursing again he could have, for I was at his place at pretty much the same time every day, give or take ten minutes. Though I would see him out in the fields working, stacking cordwood or leading the cows back to the barn, he never lay in wait for me, or acknowledged me when I waved, and I took this as a sign that we had reached some kind of peace or, perhaps, that I had earned his respect.

As it turned out, Wallace told me later, he was simply not as engaged in the struggle over the delivery of the mail as I thought he was. He hated the mail, that was true, and did not want it brought to him, but if I was so determined to put it on his door, then so be it. He simply put it in the pile of trash to be burned.

As fall turned to winter, and the snow began to fly, I got my first taste of difficult driving. The Jeep was four-wheel drive, and generally solid, though it was a boxy car, and thus not especially well-balanced. It seemed particularly suited for deep snow, which it got out of with no trouble, but sometimes coming down the steep hillsides of Eden I felt the wheels slide underneath me and had to constantly correct it so as not to fishtail.

The week before Christmas, we had our first serious snowstorm of the season. It was a Monday, and by the time I had reached the general store and begun to load the plastic cartons of mail into the Jeep, eight inches had fallen. Connie told me to take it easy out there, she had heard on the police scanner she listened to all day that there were accidents all over the place. 'It's that real greasy snow,' she said.

The going was slow as most of the roads had not yet been plowed, and even though I felt the Jeep slipping here and there, by and large I worked through my route without any troubles. I was coming down the steep hill before Wallace Fiske's house when that all changed. The hill before Wallace's had a sharp hairpin turn at the end, one that, if you did not know it was there, was so sharp that even in good weather it was difficult to stay on the road. The only way to handle it, as best I could tell, was to downshift to first at the top of the hill and let the natural braking of the engine slow the Jeep down enough that you could ease into it. This time, as I downshifted from second to first, I felt the Jeep slip beneath me, and before I knew it I was sideways and, trying to compensate, I drove in the direction of the skid, but this made it worse, and somehow I made it around the hairpin turn on the shoulder, snow flying up and into the windshield blinding my vision. But then suddenly I was airborne, the Jeep leaving the road and plummeting down the steep ravine that led to Wallace's land.

I came to a stop next to a tree. The front end of the Jeep was deep in the snow, so that I could not see out, and I had the sense that the back wheels were elevated, a suspicion that would later turn out to be correct. I felt something warm on my head and, when I pushed my hand across my forehead, it was wet with blood. I had banged my head pretty hard on the windshield.

What followed was a time of relative incoherence. I had a sense of snow, wet, sticky snow, piling on the Jeep, on me, obscuring me. I wondered when someone would realize I had not returned the Jeep and come looking for me. It was hard to imagine whether I was even visible from the road. I drifted in and out of dreams. I dreamt that I was running, running through the forest, something moving quickly behind me, but I was agile and fast, leaping over fallen timber and heavy brush, jumping perfectly between the forked branches of a giant tree, and then, comfortable that I had shaken whatever it was that hunted me, I lay down to rest on a soft forest floor of ferns, the leaves tickling my cheeks, bringing me to deep slumber.

Something was tugging on my arm. My head felt heavy. Lift it, I told myself. Lift and look. Something was in my eyes. My head ached, ached real bad. Felt as if it was in a vise. I heard a voice. A deep voice. Speak up, I said, or did I? Could I say that? Could I say anything? I wanted to sleep, wanted to sleep more than anything. Curl up under heavy sheets and shut my eyes.

'Relax,' the voice said. 'Let me get you out of here.'

That's better, I thought; now at least you are talking out loud. My arms were being tugged again, and this time it hurt, and I shouted, 'Fuck,' but then I felt the cold, cold snow, snow on my back, in my pants, on my arms, and I remember laughing then, laughing because I was lying in snow and this I knew, could comprehend, could comprehend with my own two eyes, for a minute or two, anyway, and then I was out again, floating on that soft bed of ferns.

I CAME to in a low-ceilinged room, cracks like spiderwebs emanating from a heat grate in the center. I was on a bed, a single bed, wood frame. The covers were heavy. The room was lit by an oil lamp on a table next to the door. The walls were a light green, but the paint was chipped badly, plaster visible. There was a small window to my left, and it was dark, but somewhere there was a light, and I could see the snow falling outside in sheets like rain. I had a sharp pain in my head, like a deep migraine, but other than that all I felt were the familiar pangs of hunger.

After a while the door to the room opened and there stood Wallace Fiske, filling the frame, wearing a jacket and jeans and peering at me from beneath his heavy brow. In his hands he held a plate, and he brought it over to me, placing it next to me. He then put his hand on my forehead and held it there for a minute. He picked up the plate and put it on my lap.

'You should eat,' he said.

The plate had small pieces of dark meat on it and nothing else.

'It's venison,' he said.

I looked up at him. From up close the lines in his face were deep furrows, grooved like the trunk of an old tree. His deepset eyes were a clear, cobalt blue, but the whites were yellowish and rheumy with age and, perhaps, drink. His nose was broad and strong, and his lips were thin, his front teeth had a prominent gap. My initial reaction when delivering the mail months ago that he was once handsome held up: he had the powerful face of a man who knew who he was.

I said, 'How long have I been here?'

'Since yesterday.'

'Am I okay?'

'You have a concussion. Some cuts and bruises. You're fine. You should eat.'

My eyes turned to the plate on my lap. I took a piece of the venison and put it in my mouth. The meat was warm and chewy. As I ate, Wallace turned and left the room, and later, after I fell asleep again, I woke briefly as he took the plate back, turning off the oil lamp on his way out.

AND THAT is how it began. As Wallace said, I was fine. The next morning I found my boots and jacket hanging from a hook in the kitchen. I was tired and hurting still, but I could walk, and outside in the bright sunshine I was surprised to see that the postal Jeep was parked in Wallace's driveway and, though the front end was bashed in, it started up when I turned the key. Wallace was nowhere to be seen, though he could have been in the barn. I found it hard to imagine that he had been able to pull the Jeep out of where it lay flush against a tree at the bottom of that narrow ravine. But that is precisely what he did, hitching a chain to its bumper and jerking it out of there with his pickup. For a man of his age, Wallace was capable of things that were always surprising me.

In a few days, the only evidence of my accident was the scar on my forehead where I had connected with the windshield. The town had the Jeep fixed, though I was forced to withstand a lot of ribbing about my flatlander driving skills. A week later, I brought Wallace a bottle of scotch and, though he was gruff and did not want to take it, I insisted, saying he had saved my life, which he scoffed at, but soon we were drinking and sometimes when men drink together they find common ground, if only in the taste of liquor. It became a regular thing that winter. Wallace and I became the unlikeliest of friends. It could have been the deep, abiding loneliness we both felt. When I think about it now, though, I think that we may have needed each other. We were each running from something. I was running from my father's death and from the shallowness of a life incomplete without shiny, new love. Wallace was running from something far more profound: a past that haunted him, a past he could not escape, and a story he had never told to anyone. It was a story he was prepared to take to the grave with him, but then I came along, and for a reason I can only chalk up to fate, he decided to tell it to me.

2

Many nights that winter Wallace and I had dinner, and he surprised me by being a capable, if not particularly fancy, cook. Having worked so long waiting tables, I knew quite a bit about food, and though his cuisine, if you could call it that, was rustic and simple, in terms of taste I would have put it up against that of any of Boston's most exclusive restaurants. I think perhaps it was the simple fresh ingredients, the venison from the woods, freshly smoked bacon from last fall's pig, chickens raised and slaughtered in the barn, fish from the pond caught with a line through the ice, canned vegetables from the previous season's garden, mushrooms gathered from the base of old trees and dried.

We ate in front of the woodstove, like an old married couple, plates on our laps, Wallace drinking his scotch, me with a glass of wine. Through the large windows we could watch the snow falling on days that it did, or watch the clear, blue winter sky turn to darkness on days that it did not. We ate in silence, each of us alone with his thoughts, the day's work behind us. My delivering of the mail, my afternoon spent in a car, driving the back roads I knew so well. Wallace's spent on the farm he had always known, each day the same, each day slightly different, all of it work that I knew, without him telling me, he had never thought much about: it was something he had always done, something he would always do, as long as his heart beat in his chest and his legs would take him where he needed to go. For a man in his late seventies, Wallace Fiske still had the vigor of someone half his age.

After dinner, we smoked, me with my Marlboros, Wallace with his pipe. It was during this time, full from dinner, flushed with alcohol, that we talked. Those first months, I did the majority of the talking. I told Wallace about my childhood in Boston, about my father's recent death, about my mother's death when I was a child, how I grew up feeling largely on my own, independent before a boy should be, yet never fully adjusting to the expectations put upon me by others. But, mostly, I told Wallace about the women I had been with, the women I had always used to define me, to track time by, benchmarks for periods of my life.

I told him about Beth, curly-haired and slightly chubby, but with a laugh that fell like water, and a deep passion that exceeded that of any woman I had ever known. I told him about Cathy, the older waitress, who seemed grateful simply to have a warm body against hers when she woke in the morning. I told him about Ginny, sexy, slender Ginny, with cat eyes and a penchant for risky sex, always wanting to make love in the back of a public bus, or in the park in the middle of the day, where the tourists on Swan Boats, should they have fixed their gaze on the bushes along the pond, might have seen her astride me, her long skirt flowing around me, sometimes catching the breeze. I told him about Eve, Eve of Vietnamese descent, a great beauty with razor sharp cheekbones, almond skin, and coal black hair down to her waist, a Boston University graduate student who, when we made love, lay passively beneath me, her eyelids fluttering slightly when I moved above her. I told him about Carrie, crazy, irrational Carrie, Carrie who used to climb up the fire escape to my apartment, jimmy the window, and be waiting in my closet when I came home from my shift, emerging like some naked apparition as I went to turn the lights off, refusing to let me sleep until she had left scratches on my back. I told him about Diana, the figure skater, who woke at the crack of dawn and left me sleeping so that she could dance on ice. I told him about Tara, lithe and redheaded and freckle-faced, whose lilting Irish accent threatened to break my heart every time she opened her mouth. I even told him about a girl whose name I don't remember, a girl I met in a bar in the shadow of Fenway Park, a girl who took me back to her apartment on the top floor of an old house near Cleveland Circle and then let all her birds – six or seven of them – out of their cages to fly around the small room while she undressed. I told him how I could not sleep if there was even one moth in my room and how I left there faster than I had come in, spending the night walking the blue streets of Boston in the rain.

I talked about my serial monogamy, about how I could not find a way to make love stay. I told him what my last girl-friend, Jill, the divinity student, so wisely said to me. She said, 'Nathan, you're very good at making women fall in love with you. The only problem is you don't know what to do with them when they get there.'

I told Wallace how I used to fall in love hundreds of times a week on city sidewalks. Sometimes it was little more than a glance, or a woman I sat across from on the subway, but it did not take much for me to feel smitten and, regardless of what relationship I was in, the remainder of the day I would dwell on the particulars of that woman's face, her eyes, her mouth, her nose, her hair. Wallace rightly pointed out that this hardly qualified as love, but how else to explain it? How else to explain how a strange woman could so get under my skin and into my brain that I thought about nothing else but her for hours? A woman I had never so much as spoken to?

Perhaps it was that I was more attuned, more sensitive to beauty than others. That I felt it viscerally, in my bones. But I knew in my heart the beauty I saw was like so much flotsam on top of the ocean, never dipping below the surface. More than anything this admission revealed a shallowness of char-acter about which I could not be proud and, equally troubling, could not seem to shed.

For his part, Wallace was a good listener. Sometimes he smiled, sometimes he laughed, but mostly he sat across from me drawing on his pipe, his face resting on his left hand, his long fingers sagely pointing toward his mouth. He never offered me advice, or even commented much on what I told him, but occasionally I could see him looking out the window, and the look in his eyes confused me, his eyes slightly moist, glassy, as if he were somewhere else; looking back on it now I realize that I had touched a nerve, had triggered some of his own memories. At the time, though, I had the common naïveté of youth, in which you see life only as it appears to you that very moment, and I never imagined Wallace as anything other than what he was right then, an old man with rheumy eyes and a need for companionship, something concrete to take away the chill of the quiet nights before death. Just as it was difficult for me to imagine myself as someday becoming Wallace – the cigarette in my hand, for instance, a burning symbol of my youthful sense of immortality – so, too, it was difficult for me to understand that Wallace had once been young like me, had once loved and lost, had once taken the strength of his body for granted. It was not until his own story began to unfold that I realized how much he, like me, had done all those things.

ONCE AGAIN it was car trouble that led me deeper into Wallace's world. Winter had given way to April, and with April in Eden came mud season, Vermont's fifth season. An entire winter's frost released itself to those dirt roads and, for a few staggering weeks, the roads were the consistency of whipped chocolate, making driving difficult at best, nearly impossible at worst. After a few days of this, they developed well-worn ruts, and in places the mud was like quicksand, so that you would start spinning your wheels and, before you knew it, all four tires were buried in the road.

I was about a half mile before Wallace's house, and I still had to negotiate the steep hill, which was in some ways safer during mud season because, no matter how fast you tried to drive, the mud would slow you down. It might spin you around, but chances were it would keep you on the road. As I crested the small rise before that sharp descent, however, I saw the thick grooves in the road below, and in the grooves I saw where water had pooled up in small streams that were being fed from a natural culvert coming out of the woods. I knew it would be a tricky spot, so I picked up speed to try to motor my way through, but as I reached it I had that old feeling of fishtailing, and I braced myself, but the Jeep corrected itself and then simply stopped. I revved the engine, but the wheels stubbornly dug in. I slipped it into reverse and accelerated quickly and then just as fast put it into first and accelerated again, vainly trying to get the Jeep rocking. Mud kicked up from the road and splattered the windshield. I tried again. But it was no use, I felt myself digging deeper and deeper.

I got out of the Jeep. The mud was up over the wheel wells. I walked around it, checking all sides. I was stuck solid. There was no way I was getting out without a tow.

I left the Jeep in the middle of the road and began to walk down the hill toward Wallace's place. The sky was a pale blue above the tree-lined road and in the sun it was warm, but when the wind picked up you still felt the lingering chill of winter in its breath. Through the trees I saw patches of snow still on the ground, and all around I heard water, seasonal streams gushing high through the woods with snowmelt. My feet made deep impressions in the soft road as I walked.

When I reached Wallace's place, I was relieved to see his pickup in the driveway. But he was nowhere to be seen. I looked in the house, calling out for him. No answer. Next I walked across the pasture where the small herd of Jerseys looked at me with their doe eyes as I passed. I opened the large doors to the barn. It was dark in there, but as my eyes adjusted I realized that it, too, was empty. I went around the front of the house and looked down the stretch of land to the pond below, my eyes scanning the low-brush pastures and thin trees around it for any sign.

I was about to give up when across the road from his house I spied Wallace's dog through the trees. He stood partway up a thin trail that led through the dense forest. The dog saw me as I entered the trail and glared at me, yellow-toothed and snarling, but when I got closer recognized me and gave me a sad, aged attempt at a tail wag.

I rubbed his head. 'What's up, boy? Where's your master?'

If the dog knew, he was not saying. I left him and continued on the trail, which was easy going at first but then got steeper, taking me up the side of the forest wall. Soon I had reached the top of the hill, and the trees opened almost immediately to a surprisingly large expanse of field and pasture. I stopped and turned around.

Below now I could see Wallace's house, a thin plume of

smoke rising up from the chimney, and beyond that I could see the blueness of Mirror Lake and then the mountains in the distance. On the trail, the dog slowly ambled his old body toward me.

The day was warm now and the field itself, in sharp contrast to the softness of the road and the marshiness of the woods, was dry, and the brush crunched slightly under my feet as I began to walk across it, heading toward the forest on the far side. This was beautiful Vermont land, slightly rolling but flat enough to build on, with 360-degree views. In fact, it struck me that if you were to build on Wallace's land today this would most likely be where you would do it, cut a driveway in from the woods, place a house back on the flat of the land near the trees, with a porch to the range of bluish mountains.

As I reached the center of the field, the land began to slope slightly downward again, and I saw now that the field continued on farther than I had previously thought, doglegging like a golf course around a grove of tall evergreens. I don't know what made me think that this was where Wallace was, but for some reason I felt drawn to go there, to stride across this field, with my Jeep buried in mud a half mile up the road, the early spring sun now warm on my neck, the sound of rushing water growing louder as I got closer to the woods.

My instincts proved correct. No sooner had I come around the corner of the trees than I saw Wallace at the end of the field, a couple of hundred yards from where I was, down one-kneed on the ground, his face against his upright knee. In front of him was a leafless apple tree, stark against the deep green woods, and beyond that a wooded hill rose up against the blue sky.

He looked ill, as if he'd had a stroke, which I had never seen before but imagined it might look like, as if Wallace had been walking when it struck like lightning, and took him to one knee.

I thought about calling out, but something inside me told me not to, and so I began instead to walk slowly toward him. Wallace remained absolutely motionless. I walked carefully, one foot in front of the other, trying not to make any noise. I knew for some reason that I was witnessing something I should not, something that did not belong to me but something, as well, that I could not turn away from.

When I was about fifty yards from Wallace, I stopped. Directly in front of him, on the ground, a white granite headstone rose up out of the base of the apple tree. Leaning against the headstone was a solitary flower, and when I listened I heard what sounded like muffled sobs coming from Wallace's throat.

I stood stock-still, watching his back, not wanting him to see me. His cries were audible now, and he began to rock slightly back and forth where he crouched. At one point he reached across and took the headstone in his hands, but then he went quickly back to kneeling the way he was, his hands covering his face.

I stood there for a total of probably two or three minutes, but it seemed like hours. I, too, have grieved in my life, too often for a man of my age, and know the empty feeling you get when you stand in front of the representation of a person – in this case, a headstone – and try to recall their flesh, their blood, their life. When my father died I delivered the eulogy, which was difficult, but in truth it was only words, an academic exercise of sorts, and I was able to get through it without any trouble. When they lowered him into the ground, however, and the small clump of dirt left my palm and hit the dark, shiny wood of the coffin, sliding off it in tiny granules, the sense of pathos washed over me like a wave and I fell to my knees, the emptiness of it all too much for me to handle standing up.

I know that very few people handle death and its mysteries well, but I was worse equipped than most, largely because I found living so mysterious and never seemed, as I have said before, to be able to live purposefully. The way I handled death – except, as in the case of my father, where the choice did not exist – was to avoid it altogether, to keep it out of conversation, out of thought, and certainly out of sight. Now, watching another man grieve for I knew not whom, I felt guilty for my avoidance, my inability to face things head-on. And, more directly, I wondered who it was that lay amongst the old roots of that tree.

Eventually I walked back the way I came, across the long expanse of meadow to the path through the woods, past Wallace's dog, now lying in a patch of burdock, to the road and past Wallace's house.

The upshot of it all was that, when I reached the Jeep, it had already been towed out by someone who could not get by, and was now sitting on firm land on the side of the road, ready for me to continue my route, which I did, my mind full of questions about Wallace Fiske, about a grave at the end of the field, and it occurred to me as I passed Mirror Lake in my Jeep, the wind blowing the surface into a light chop, if you knew what it was a man grieved for, in many ways you knew what it was he lived for.

3

Mud season passed and the roads eventually hardened and the town tractors came by and graded them back as smooth as tar. And for two weeks I drove right past Wallace's house without stopping, for I was concerned that if I talked to him he would see it in my face, my guilt at having seen something I should not have.

During that time I never saw Wallace once, not outside with his cows, or down by the lake fishing for trout. I saw signs of him, cans of paint by the door, the fishing rod leaning against the side of the porch, the cows in a different pasture than the afternoon before.

As for me, I took advantage of my newfound loneliness to return to my old ways. I started frequenting the one pub in town, a small hole in the wall next to the general store where

men gathered to drink Budweiser and watch sports on television and talk. Within days I had slipped right into the group
of regulars – farmers and loggers and contractors – as if I had
been there all my life. It was a chameleonlike quality that I
had, to relate to different people, to fit in, and collectively they
filled the void that had been opened in my evenings. Often I
arrived after dinner, driving the postal Jeep, and left when the
lights went on at the end of the night, drunk on beer and
sometimes some whiskey, coughing from an evening of inces-
santly smoking Marlboros. In the mornings I woke with a big
head but managed to do my route, take a nap, eat dinner, and
then do it again. The days developed a new rhythm, albeit an
unhealthy one, and my life in the hills went on.

The bartender at the pub was an old man with permanent
stubble and an appetite for unfiltered cigarettes that made me
feel good about my own habit. He went by the name of Linger,
and he drank only Cokes but lit cigarette after cigarette and
coughed a raspy cough while he smoked. Everyone liked
Linger in the way people like things they can rely on, and in
truth he was as nice a man as you will ever meet. Good and
solid and kind. But one night when I arrived, Linger was gone,
taken to the hospital, people said, and a hat was passed for
him, and his daughter, a thin, mousy girl with stringy blond
hair, had taken over the bartending duties.

At first I did not think much of her, but as the night
progressed I noticed that she had a soft, shy smile that I found
endearing. She was one of those women that the longer you
look at her, the more she grows on you. I watched her move
behind the bar, tapping a new keg, washing glasses, reaching

up to change the channel on the television, and as she did I began to imagine her body beneath her clothes.

The following night I struck up a conversation with her. Her name was Kate, and during the days she worked as a teller at the bank. I asked how fast she could count money, and she opened the register and showed me, the bills shuffling quickly through her hands, sorting by denomination.

'Nice,' I said.

We ended talking late into the night, long after the place had closed, and I helped put up the stools and sweep the floors. We went back to my place where, while the moonlight painted stripes on the walls of my room, I moved gently inside her. We made love off and on until the sun rose, and she was not beautiful but she was willing and it had been a long time since I had held the curved back of a woman in my hands and I was grateful for it. I had almost forgotten what a gift it was.

And so it was that I was back where I was before I came to Eden, shutting out the outside noise by falling into the arms of another new woman. Linger came back to work, and Kate stopped going to the bar, as did I, for now I spent all the time I could with her.

One Sunday, when neither of us had to work, we never left bed, making love with the sun shining through the big storefront windows of my bedroom, looking out over the rolling hills of Eden toward the purple horn of Camels Hump. After a while she slept, I rested my head in the crook of her neck and pressed my lips softly against her collarbone and ran my hands across the soft table of her belly. When she woke I told her I loved her, and she laughed for she was smart enough to know it was not true, and intuitive enough to see right through my flimsy veneer of infatuation, and when I rose up on elbows above her and looked her in the eyes as if to say, What? she smiled and said, 'Why don't you just tell the truth? You love fucking me.'

'Oh, is that right?' I said.

'I like you better when you don't talk,' she said and pulled me down on top of her, and once again I was inside of her and the world fell away outside the windows, and it was only the two of us, on a bed like an altar, suspended in the blue sky above the green hills of Eden.

THEN, ON a humid May afternoon when a warm, spring rain pounded onto the tin roof of my cabin, I was inside making spaghetti sauce when I heard a knock at the door.

'Hold on,' I called out, and wiped my hands on a towel and turned down the burner on the stove and went to the door expecting to see Kate, though she was not supposed to be here for another hour. Instead, when I looked through the glass window of the door I saw a familiar tall figure in a Carhartt jacket standing on the porch. The rain poured off his head, matting his hair to his forehead. He looked tired, and he shrugged when he saw me. I opened the door.

'Wallace,' I said.

'Hello, Nathan.'

'Jesus, what are you doing here?'

'Can I come in? It's awfully wet out here.'

'Of course.'

I stepped aside and let him into my small kitchen.

'This is my place,' I said.

Wallace looked around, nodded. He opened his coat and took out a bottle of Highland scotch and handed it to me and I put it on the table.

I said, 'Have a seat.'

Wallace sat on a chair at the table. He wiped his brow with his sleeve, and I said, 'Let me take your coat,' and he stood and slipped it off and handed it to me. I placed it on one of the rungs of the ladder leading up to my bedroom and then sat down across from him. I looked at him.

'You look like shit,' I said.

'Then give me a drink.'

I got two glasses and cracked the bottle and filled us each about three generous fingers. Wallace took his glass and brought it to his lips. He took one long swallow, and I watched his Adam's apple bob.

'I know you were there,' he said.

'Where?'

'On the hill. The grave site.'

I looked away. 'I didn't know you saw me.'

'I didn't. It was your boots. The tracks on the path. Footprints.'

Wallace sighed and sat back in his chair. He took another pull off his glass of scotch. Then he reached into the breast pocket of his shirt and pulled something out. He handed it across to me.

It was a photograph, black and white and old. In the foreground was a woman in a white dress, and she had dark hair around a face that would have been plain if it were not for her eyes, which were exceptional, deep and dark and spaced far apart, and for her smile, which was wide and blissful. I could almost imagine what her laughter sounded like. She sat curled on a blanket with a bottle of beer in her hand and behind her, in the background, was a man in a white suit and dark tie, sitting awkwardly, his knees bunched up toward his chest. By contrast, the look on his face was stoic, reserved. In between them was a picnic basket, and I got a sense of summer, grass and sky.

'Who is she?'

'Nora.'

'Nora?'

'My wife.'

I looked more closely at the photograph, and I now saw clearly that the man in the background was a young Wallace, his strong jaw, a lock of hair falling down toward his eyes. How it was not apparent to me right away I did not know, except that sometimes looking at a picture like that is like looking at a mosaic, it can take a moment before it fully reveals itself. I did not know what to say.

I said, 'She's beautiful.'

'Yes, she was.'

I turned the photograph over. On the back someone had written '1947.'

'She's the one by the apple tree,' I said.

'Yes.'

'When did she die?'

'A long times ago.'

'I didn't know you were married.'

'It's not something I talk about.'

Wallace took his pipe out of his pocket then, and looked at me questioningly, and I knew that he wanted to talk. I nodded and then watched as he filled his pipe with tobacco and brought it to his lips and lit it, inhaling quickly, the pungent smoke spilling out of his mouth and into the room. I was curious and anxious to hear what he wanted to say, what it was he wanted to tell me, and I realized that all these months when I had done the talking it never dawned on me that he had stories of his own.

I leaned back and sipped my scotch. Outside the rain had intensified, a hard, driving rain, water pooling up on the wooden porch.

'That is the only picture I have of her,' Wallace said. 'It is my most valuable possession. You know how people ask what is the one thing you'd save if the house is on fire and you only have a minute to get out? For me, it's that picture. It was taken the summer we met. The summer my father died and I was alone on the farm. I didn't work as hard as I should have that summer. And it was because of her, because of Nora.

'I remember that day the photo was taken. Remember it clearly. It was late summer and there was work to do, lots of it, the farm was much bigger then, busier. But Nora had a way of talking me out of things. 'The work will wait,' she said. Next thing we're up in the field, where you saw me, where that apple tree is, only it wasn't there yet. She planted it later because that spot was special to her. We had a blanket, some beer, cheese, bread. I know to you a picnic sounds like no big deal, but to someone like me then, to do it in the middle of the day like that, in late summer with so much work to do – it was practically madness.'

I smiled. 'Sounds like it was worth it.'

Wallace looked toward the window again, the rain falling hard against the glass. 'I had never felt that way before. We talked, we ate, we looked at the pond. But we also sat in silence, sat and said nothing. I liked that the best. The not talking. Hard to explain. Silence is probably the wrong word. Because I realized we could sit together and not say anything but it was more than silence. Not sound either. I know that sounds crazy.'

I thought about it. 'I can see that,' I said, and I could, theoretically, though I had never experienced it, having always been somehow afraid of silence when with a woman, trying as hard as I could to fill the air.

Wallace said, 'We were in love. No question about it. From the moment I saw her at a dance at the Grange in the village, what is now that guy's house, the guy who drives a Mercedes.'

I nodded. I knew the house; it was on my route and a Mercedes in Eden was as rare as a herd of cows in Boston. I said, 'Baker. Milton Baker.'

'Right. I never went to those things, but for some reason that night I did. Clear night, early spring, and I remember how high the water was running over the mill. It filled the whole town with the sound of it. Back then we used to have these dances there, some Friday nights. It wasn't much. People drank, smoked, talked. A fiddle band played, sometimes some horns. There was dancing, not by me of course. I wasn't much of a dancer. But I was single then and, unlike you, I was actively looking for a wife. My father was dying, my mother was dead, and the farm was more than one man could handle then. So I went. And for the first time, I saw Nora. She was the new schoolteacher, filling in halfway through the year for a woman who had gotten hitched. My eyes lit on her right away. She was dancing when I came in, being swung around by a partner, and her dress was catching the air, flowing up around her legs, her long hair behind her. God, she was a sight. Right then I knew I would marry her.'

I stopped him. 'How could you be so certain?'

Wallace took a long pull of his pipe. He smiled. 'Some things you just know. If you're lucky, Nathan, you'll figure that out. Trust your instincts. You know how you can feel snow in the air before it comes? Sometimes before even the sky goes gray, you can feel it, somewhere between your heart and your head. And it's not experience talking either. It's inborn. Cows have it, so do birds. And people do as well, though they don't always listen to it. And seeing her, I knew it. I saw our lives coming together, I saw us growing old together. I saw it all in the amount of time it takes for a door to open, and she hadn't even so much as seen me yet.'

I thought about that. Every time I met a woman I felt an immediate certainty that this was the one, only to have that certainty fade as quickly as it came on. The pattern for me was predictable: infatuation, illusory love, then I began to have doubts, dwell on flaws, become disillusioned. And, inevitably, I left.

I said, 'What did you do?'

'Nothing that night. I watched her. I caught her eye from where I stood with some other farmers drinking, but that was about it. I watched her dance. And you can tell a lot about a woman from the way she dances. The way she moves. How comfortable she is in her own skin. And Nora was an incredible dancer. It came easily to her. She danced the entire night, and the entire night I watched her. That night, lying in my bed, I thought about her. I slept terribly. Tossed and turned, and the next morning my eyes were red-rimmed when I rose to do the milking, but I was at peace because one of my major challenges – finding a wife – felt complete.'

I shook my head at this. 'When did you see her next?'

'Not for two weeks. I thought about her until the thinking became too much and I had to do something about it. So I showed up at the schoolhouse in the middle of the afternoon when the children were leaving. And I waited for her and asked if I could walk her home. She lived in a boardinghouse on Foster Hill. She knew who I was, in the roundabout way that everyone in Eden knew everyone then. It's a little different now. Anyway, we walked and we talked and, when we reached the door to the house she was staying in, I asked if I could see her again. I'll never forget what she said.'

'What?'

'Absolutely not.' Wallace laughed.

I gave him a puzzled look.

'And then when I looked completely aghast, she said, "I'm only giving you a hard time, Wallace. I'd like that."'

'And that's how you met.'

'That's how we met.'

I stood up. 'I need to check the spaghetti sauce,' I said and went to the stove and stirred it. Outside, the rain had let up a little, though it was now dark so it was hard to tell. I looked at the clock, six-thirty. I wondered when Kate would show up. I had not yet told Wallace about her.

I said, 'Did you start seeing each other right away?'

Wallace, with his back to me, refilled his glass of scotch. 'It was a slow courtship. Every day I met her at the end of the school day and I walked her back to the house. I did this for almost a month. I'd like to think my intentions were clear, but of course I only made them clear by being there. We never talked about it. She never told me not to come, so I did, religiously, standing at the door of the very place I went to school, waiting for the teacher. We would walk slowly back, and sometimes I would take her hand and hold it in my own. One time I asked her if she could meet me at night for a walk. This was in May.'

I sat back down, lit a cigarette. The rain had picked up again, pounding hard on the tin roof. 'And she did?'

'Oh, yes. I met her at the base of Foster Hill, and the sun was going down. We walked through the village again, retracing our daily walk from the school, only this time we turned up my road. We walked to the pond, and we stopped at the clearing on the road and sat down on a log, our feet dangling down above the water. It was a full moon and the loons were out on the pond and we could hear their voices. We sat in silence for a while. Gradually I put my arm around her. Then, after a while, I leaned over and kissed her. And she kissed me back. And we sat kissing in the dark with our feet over the water. And for weeks we did that. Met at night and walked to the same spot and sat on that log and looked across the pond to where you could see the lights on my house and we kissed. We barely ever talked then. We held hands, we kissed, but other than that we listened to the loons and the night sounds. It was a lovely time.'

Wallace stopped, looked out the window into the dark, took a sip of his scotch, and I saw that his eyes were moist. I was about to say something when the door opened and Kate came in, her blond hair wet against her head, holding a bag of groceries.

'Hello, there,' she said.

'Wallace,' I said, 'this is Kate.'

Wallace nodded and went to his feet and Kate said, 'Don't get up,' but he was already on his way, and he stood, his tall frame amplified by the smallness of the ceiling. I watched as he leaned down and took her hand. Kate then brought the groceries to the counter next to the stove and, as I turned to help her, I heard the door and looked back quickly enough to see Wallace moving out and into the night. I said, 'Wallace, wait,' but he was gone, faster than a shadow, embers from his pipe still burning in the ashtray.

THAT NIGHT, lying in bed, I told Kate what Wallace had told me. When I had finished, she said, 'That's a beautiful story.'

'Surprising.'

She looked at me, arched an eyebrow. She was naked under the sheets, and her breasts rose up slightly above the comforter, like those of some actress from a sixties French film. 'You think you invented passion, Nathan?'

I laughed. 'Of course not. It's hard to see Wallace in that light, that's all. He seems like a guy who would never have time for love.'

Kate said, 'My grandparents are over eighty and they act like newlyweds. Last summer I was at their house and it was almost ten in the morning and they still weren't out of bed. I got concerned and I was about to knock on the door when I heard the sounds of their lovemaking.'

'That's nasty,' I said.

She playfully smacked me on the arm. 'It's beautiful.'

'Yeah, well, some people shouldn't be getting it on. Old flesh and old bones moving together. Doesn't do it for me.'

She rolled away from me. 'You're so shallow. You miss the point entirely. Good night.' She reached up then and turned off the light.

I rolled into her, spooning her. I knew she was pretending to be mad, and she was, for I began to tickle her, and she slapped at my hands, saying 'Stop it,' but soon she had rolled on top of me, and as I entered her, my hands cupping her breasts, her hands pressing down on my chest, my heart, I could see that the rain had stopped, the sky had cleared, and the stars shone brightly in the moonless night. I could see the evergreens at the perimeter of the open yard, trees of different heights, my own personal skyline.

When Kate had fallen asleep, snoring softly next to me, I returned to Wallace's story. I imagined the Eden of fifty years ago, smaller and insular, a farm community defined by its sharp hills and narrow valleys but, more definitively, defined by its determined people, people like Wallace and Nora, young and in love, their lives rooted in the landscape and in each other. I saw them sitting on that log at the edge of the pond, holding hands, their feet dangling, the dying sunlight cutting a dappled path across the water to where they sat. I saw the way they looked at one another, the solidity of their kisses. And I imagined the certainty they must have felt, the certainty that Wallace had spoken of, the belief that they were meant to be together, that their lives were entwined, that nothing could ever come between them.

4

At the post office the next morning, I was loading up the Jeep when Connie came out the back door for a smoke. The day was warm and the sun bright and, though it was early, the blackflies were already out, and I could see them in front of my face, small clouds of them, no bigger than gnats. Connie had a halo of them around her head.

I said, 'How long do these fucking things last?'

She laughed. 'Until July.'

'Get out of here.'

'Relax, Nathan, I'm kidding. Another week, tops. Have a cigarette, they're nonsmokers. It helps.'

I put the last bin of mail in the back of the Jeep and joined her. I took a cigarette from her proffered pack and lit it, inhaling deeply. I looked out over the small dirt parking lot, toward where the outcropping of rock ledge hung over its south side. 'Without these bugs,' I said, 'this would be the best time of year.'

Connie coughed, dropped her cigarette, stepped on it, then just as quickly lit another. 'How's your friend, Wallace?'

'Did you know he was married?'

'Oh, yeah. Nora Fiske.'

'Did you know her?'

'A little. I knew who she was, though for years she never left that house. No one saw her. Wallace was the only one who came to town. I remember her vaguely from when I was young. She was around more then. Beautiful woman. People couldn't understand what she was doing with Wallace.'

'I've seen a picture. She was pretty.'

'She stood out here. I remember my father talking about her once and provoking an argument with my mother.'

'Because he liked her?'

Connie shrugged. 'All the men liked her. Of course this was like forty years ago, before my time even. Then she disappeared from view. Sometimes people said they saw her walking down by the pond there, or working out in the garden. She had a real green thumb. That whole area around Wallace's house was filled with perennials once. Roses that you would not believe. Bushes as high as your head. All colors, too. That place was something.'

I stubbed out my cigarette with my foot. 'Do you know what happened to her?'

'No. I mean, I heard stories. But nothing firm. People said Wallace kept her on a short leash. I also heard that she may have been a little crazy, but I don't know that that's true. Hard to blame her if she was. Putting up with Wallace all the time. Cranky asshole that he is.'

'He's not so bad.'

'Yeah, well, that's what you say, Nathan. But one thing I know about Eden: people say a lot of stuff about each other here. And not all of it's true. But after a while, when everyone says the same thing, you begin to think there might be something to it. And with Wallace, people been saying the same thing for as long as I can remember.'

I said, 'Time to go, Connie. Thanks for the smoke.'

'The mail waits for no one, Nathan. The Postal Service is a cruel mistress, don't you forget it.'

'A real bitch, Connie, a real bitch.'

I HAVE never seen a more beautiful place than Eden, Vermont, in early summer. They say that winter comes unannounced in Vermont, but for me the warning signs are there, the trees shaking off their leaves, the ponds icing over, the geese flying in Vs above in the sky. Summer, by contrast, comes with a suddenness that will stop you in your tracks, cause you to look around with something approaching wonder. So it was for me that year driving the back roads delivering the mail. One day it was spring, the ground soft underfoot, dirty snow still in the woods, a thin membrane of ice still floating on the surface of the pond in front of Wallace's house. Then you woke to discover that summer has slipped in under the cover of darkness and wildflowers have sprung up in the pastures, the hills are a deep, lush green, ferns grow madly on the sides of the shaded roads, the woods are teeming with life, birds everywhere, their dissonant cries sometimes converging into one giant voice, filling the air with natural music. The days seemed to extend forever, the sun hanging in the sky until the last possible second, before fading gracefully behind the hills, leaving behind trails of purple and gold for the moon to chase away.

It was during this time, with winter far at my back, that I felt, for lack of a better word, most right. My life was what I had hoped for when I left Boston. It was simple. I had my cabin on the hill with views of the hills and the mountains, I had a job that could not be less complicated. And I had Kate, mousy, dirty-blond-haired Kate, Kate who seemed to expect nothing from me, so that anything I gave her, anytime I gave myself up to her, was treated as a gift.

My work ended at two, and coming home I felt comfort in the fact that the day, as defined by the light, still unfolded in front of me, long and languid. Some nights I had dinner with Wallace, some nights with Kate, and the two of them were my two separate worlds, old and young, friend and lover. The two worlds sometimes even came close to coming together, for some nights after dinner in the half-light of dusk Kate and I walked down the hill from my house and through the old village to Mirror Lake, where we stripped off our clothes and swam in the cool water, floating on our backs like otters, watching the stars appear in the sky like a myriad of winking eyes. We stayed out for as long as we could, the water warmer than the air, and sometimes we embraced and I took her in my arms, pulling her to me, and if it were not for the lights of the oil lamps in Wallace's windows in the knoll above the pond, I would have sworn the universe was ours alone. I was, as you can imagine, struck in those moments by the thought of Wallace and Nora. Did they ever skinny-dip as young lovers? Did they have that feeling of being alone the way I did? Was that what certainty was? Was certainty the knowledge that if everything else fell apart, pulled away, you had each other?

Walking home on the dirt roads in the lightless dark, our hair wet, the air fortunately warm enough that the chill from the water was bearable, I would take Kate's hand in my own. Together we walked, our arms swinging in unison, and sometimes she put her head on my shoulder and I wrapped my arm around her and brought her to me, held her close until we saw the headlights of a car, at which point we separated and moved to the side of the road, the car passing us without even knowing we were there, its lights vanishing around a bend in the road, leaving us alone in the dark, listening to the sounds of the brook, the sounds of the night.

ONE JUNE evening I was at Wallace's and we had finished another one of his dinners − brook trout sautéed in bacon, shallots, whiskey, and fresh garden herbs − and the two of us were sitting on his porch looking out over the expanse of Mirror Lake. The sun had set, but the sky was still a pale blue and you could see clearly the steeple from the schoolhouse rising up from between the hills in Gospel Hollow. It had been almost a month since that rainy night in my cabin when he told me about Nora and how they met. I had seen him dozens of times since and he had refrained from saying anything to me about it, and, in fact, acted as if he had never told me. Instead, our conversations tended to focus on the weather, the cows, the summer, and sometimes, when we had drunk enough scotch, I told him about Kate, how I liked her earthiness, her approach to things, how she kept me grounded.

But that night, sitting on Wallace's porch in creaky rocking chairs, smoking, I told him my fear. 'I'm worried about losing her.'

Wallace smiled. 'Maybe that's progress, Nathan.'

'What do you mean?'

'From what you've told me, I'd think you'd be worried about keeping her.'

'Good point.'

'What makes you worried?'

I looked out toward the lake. How to put this. 'It's just a sense I have. An uneasiness. In a way, I don't want to fall in love with her. But I am.'

'This from a man who says he falls in love on the subway.'

I looked at him. 'This is different.'

'How?'

'I'm not sure. I think perhaps it's because she doesn't seem to be in love with me. I'm used to being the unattainable one. Let me say that differently. It's not that she's not in love with me, it's more that she gives me the idea that she could live without me easily.'

'She could.'

'What makes you say that?'

Wallace shifted forward in his chair. 'You think you're different than any other man? You have something they don't? No. Men are the same everywhere. And sometimes we realize that too late. We are replaceable, Nathan. If not you, then someone else.'

I thought about that. It was too easy. 'Well, you could say the same thing about women.'

Wallace smiled. 'No, I don't think so. When a woman opens herself up to you, she will only do it once. If you don't seize it, it has passed. And it may never happen again, it may be your only chance. Listen, walk with me.'

Wallace stood then, and I followed. He walked down the steps of his porch and onto the lawn. The crescent-shaped moon was high in the sky above the hills now, and the darkness was thin so that we could see clear across the lake. As we walked, I could feel the grass wet on my shoes. Wallace's dog came from underneath the porch and waddled behind us, giving up when we reached the road, turning twice before settling in a heap on the dry dirt.

Together we walked down the hill toward the lake. We walked slowly, on account of Wallace's knees, and in the distance we could hear a truck making its way slowly up Foster Hill on the other side of the pond, its gears grinding as it hit the switchbacks. We stopped at the edge of the lake, and Wallace bent and picked up a stick and tossed it toward the water. It hit the surface, sending ripples cascading out from it, and then floated, moving toward the bank. Wallace turned to me.

He said, 'What's the worst thing you've ever done?'

I looked across to the opposite shore, where the evergreens rose like a seamless dark wall across the hillside. I lit a cigarette, looked down at my shoes. 'I don't know.'

'You're hardly perfect, Nathan. I know that.'

I thought about it. Why was Wallace asking me this? On the one hand, our conversations tended to move in directions like this. On the other hand, you do not ask a question like that unless you intend for it to lead somewhere else, somehow back to you.

'Let me think,' I said. Out on the pond a fish jumped, its reentry making a loud plop. When I was in college, for a time I had been a thief. I stole a bike, shoplifted from stores, took wallets from unsuspecting students. It was a brief but heady period of larceny, when virtually anything I saw I thought about ways to make mine. And, of course, there were the girls I had dated, which I had told Wallace all about. I had not been a complete lout, at least not intentionally, though at times I had said things, done things, of which I am not proud.

I said, 'I used to steal.'

'Ever hurt anybody?'

'Physically? In a fight?'

'Yes.'

'No. I've always been afraid of fighting. Even as a kid, I did whatever it took to not get in a fight. Of course, at that age – ten or eleven – keeping from getting your ass kicked is as basic as eating. Have you? Hurt somebody?'

Wallace looked at me, smiled. He pointed with his hand. 'See the peninsula out there? Where it juts out?'

The pond was tooth-shaped and, on the far side opposite Wallace's house, a thin peninsula slid out into the water. It was dark now, but having seen it during the day I knew it was covered with scrubby brush, some small trees. I nodded. 'Yes.'

'About five feet off of that, the pond bottom falls off in a steep shelf. My father used to say there are caves down there. All I know is that it is very deep, at least two hundred feet. About five years ago some historian from Montpelier asked me if he could look down there. He had some tiny submarine he had built himself. Anyway, they found a Revolutionary War cannon and they pulled it out. It was pretty well-preserved, because it must be real cold down there. It's at the statehouse now, on display.'

'That's interesting,' I said, 'but you didn't answer my question.'

'Which was?'

'Did you ever hurt anybody?'

Wallace turned away from the water and began to move toward the house. His back was to me now and, as he started to walk slowly up the hill, he suddenly turned around and I thought I saw his eyes flash in the dark. He said, 'Have you ever seen a squirrel in a cage trap?'

'No.'

'Sometimes all of us get like that. Running back and forth, our teeth slamming against the bars of what confines us. At one time, that was me.'

Wallace turned around and started up the hill again. I finished my cigarette, looking out across the pond, a trace of moonlight cutting across its center. I started up after him, and by the time I had reached his house the oil lamps were out, the place was shut down for the night, and I drove the dirt roads to my cabin on the hill, the image of a trapped squirrel in my head, trying to figure out precisely what he meant.

5

Memory, I realize now, has a way of sorting itself into a level of coherence, a narrative, if you will, after all the essential events have taken place. It's easy for me to know now, for instance, that in our conversations Wallace was nipping around the edges of a story that he wanted me to know. But, at the time, things came out in dribs and drabs, fragments of conversation we had over meals at his house, over walks in the woods, while standing at the edge of the pond on a summer's night. It was only later, when the truth of his relationship with Nora became clear to me, that I realized it was there all along, wanting me to grasp it. In my defense, however, friendship – in this case my friendship with Wallace – has a way of clouding one's vision, of obscuring the actual nature of things.

It should be clear by now that Wallace was as inscrutable

as a cardsharp. He talked about himself reluctantly and, when he did, it was often elliptically and, in truth, I was not as good a listener then as I am now, my own youthful stories and my need to tell them, to understand them, often not allowing me to fully hear others.

When did he tell me about his wedding day? Oddly enough, I cannot be sure. Sometimes when I think about my time with Wallace, I tend to remember seemingly mundane details with remarkable clarity, while the larger stories somehow elude me. Nevertheless, the day Wallace and Nora were married went like this: It rained in the morning but, by the time they had entered the church, the sky had cleared and the fall sun shone brightly onto the foliage-filled hiss of Eden. This was early October, 1949. The wedding was timed to coincide with the ending of harvest, things being much more governed by the growing seasons than they are today. Most of the town was there, and Wallace said he was not nervous, for the same reasons he said he would marry Nora the first time he saw her. When things are meant to happen, he said, you take them as they come.

Wallace was not a churchgoer, and neither was Nora, really, though they had a simple Protestant ceremony at the church in Gospel Hollow, which now serves as the town hall. After, a caravan of cars, trucks and, yes, horses made its way up the winding dirt roads to Wallace's house. At the house, a neighbor had been busy roasting an entire pig since the previous evening. Guests brought dishes: baked beans, succotash, potatoes, roast chicken, coleslaw. But before they ate, Wallace had one thing he needed to do.

While the people of Eden stood on the front lawn of his house and clapped, he carried Nora in his arms down to the lakeshore and fulfilled a tradition that had been his father's and his father's before him. At the lake's edge he lifted her into the air and tossed her into the cold water, Nora landing on her side, going under for a moment before coming up, her long hair trailing behind her. After, he brought her back to the house and she changed and a fiddler played, and people danced. They drank beer and whiskey. The party went on until dark, when the sun had set and the night grew cool, and pretty soon it was only Wallace and Nora, and it dawned on him that for the first time she was his alone.

He jokingly carried her in his arms across the threshold, and upstairs he laid her on his bed. He thought that maybe she was afraid of him so he told her not to worry, but he realized that he was the one who was worried, who did not know what to do, and to his relief it was she that initiated things. And, for the first time in his life, in the bedroom that had been his parents', and his grandparents' before them, on a cool, fall night, Wallace Fiske made love to a woman. After, he told me, as they lay together, she suddenly got up off the bed and began to put her dress back on.

He said, 'Where are you going?'

She sat down on the bed and laughed, putting her face in her hands.

'What is it?' Wallace said.

'For a minute,' Nora said, 'I forgot that I live here.'

In a short time, the two of them had adjusted to life together on the farm. Nora quit her job teaching or, more accurately –

with a logic I still do not understand – was relieved of her teaching duties since teaching was considered then to be the province of only single women. But, as Wallace said, the farm was busier then, and he needed her help. They raised cows, sold milk, grew crops to feed the cows, kitchen gardens to feed themselves. In the early spring, when the sap ran, they sugared, and they sold the syrup. In between there was wood to cut, house repairs to be done, pigs and chickens to be raised and slaughtered, meat to be smoked. It was New England hill farm living and, though it sounds at a distance as if it was romantic, in truth it was a hard life.

But, still, Wallace recalls those early years of marriage as his happiest. As he told me one afternoon as we walked along the upper meadows of his land, 'Sometimes I'd be working and I'd come out of the barn and I'd look up and I'd see her in the window. And she'd be looking down, doing whatever it was she was doing, canning or cooking. Then she'd look up and see me and her smile would go wide and I'd give her a little wave and she'd wave back. And I remember wondering how I got by before she came along.'

Their first winter together, Wallace said, was the worst that Eden had ever seen in anyone's recollection. By Thanksgiving, it had not snowed an inch, and the pond was frozen over, and this was, in Vermont weather forecasting, seen paradoxically as a sign of a particularly bad season to come. Sure enough, when December came the snow started. There was a near blizzard that first weekend, snow piling high against the sides of the white cape, and it simply did not seem to stop, nor'easter after nor'easter coming up the coast and then colliding with cold air from the Hudson Bay, creating a once-a-century winter. Wallace had to work twice as hard when it snowed, for all the animals needed to be inside twenty-four hours a day, meaning that he was constantly cleaning their shit out of the barn, laying new hay, feeding them.

One afternoon before Christmas, it had been snowing hard since the night before, and the wind was blowing as well, so that through the windows of their house they could see the snow moving like sand dunes, forming peaked shapes against the house, flowing over the stone walls in tall piles. Then the wind would pick up and swirl and the whiteout would start, and Wallace said it was as if there were no town, no Vermont, just this window of theirs that looked onto a vast sea of whiteness.

But snow or no snow, blizzard or no blizzard, there was still work to be done. And for several days Wallace had been battling influenza, and his stomach hurt so much that he had not eaten or drunk anything but the occasional cup of hot tea. His body was weak and, though he knew he should have been in bed, he needed to feed and to milk the Jerseys. Nora offered to do it, and she could have, but if Wallace was anything he was proud, and ignorant of his own limitations so, despite her best admonitions, he set out into the half-dark of a late December afternoon, for the short walk across the meadow to the barn. He never made it.

Wallace said that you could not imagine what it was like that afternoon. He stepped out of the door and began to walk, the snow in places up to his waist and the wind blowing wickedly across the open fields. He was only twenty or so feet away from the house when the wind began to blow so hard that total whiteout happened. He remembered turning to look at the house and realizing that he could not see it, could not see anything, save for his hands and his arms, flailing out in front of him as he pressed on. He grew quickly disoriented, and though he thought at moments he could see the barn in front of him, it would disappear like a hallucination, and he was not sure which way to go.

Wallace remembers seeing the sky then. That was the weirdest thing. One minute it's total whiteout, next he can see blue, blue sky. After that, he saw little. The white seemed to close in around him, and his legs felt like they were made of iron. He does not know when he fell, but he did, lying in the snow like a snow angel, only it was not for play, the snow was falling fast and he was unconscious.

It was his illness, the flu, that took him down. But in a way, as well, the flu saved him. For he was normally so strong and so capable that Nora did not worry about him, even in weather like this, unspeakably bad weather. But on this day, according to Wallace, she was worried about him, tried to keep him from going and, when he did, gave him only an hour before she thought something might have been wrong. Under different conditions, she might have let him stay out there late, figuring he was working.

So Nora bundled up as Wallace had done, and then stepped into the white, blinding snow, the darkness having descended by this time, no lights visible save for the ones in the house behind her. She must have retraced his steps, at least his initial ones, for though there is no way either Wallace or I know this, what else would she have done? Apparently, she made it to the barn, something Wallace could not do, and when she shoved aside the large doors, she realized he was not there. She then began to walk across the meadow, the wind having subsided by now, and she must have been able to see in a way that Wallace could not, for she searched for hours across the meadow, certain that Wallace was somewhere in that snowy world, and somehow she managed not to get disoriented or lose her way. In the end she found him quite by accident, only ten feet away from the back of the house, and she found him when her foot stepped on his legs. She uncovered him and cleaned him off, and with a strength I can only imagine she was able to drag his large body through the snow and into the house.

Today if this happened in Eden, Vermont, you would call 911, as you would in most places in America and, while you might not get an ambulance right away, you would at least get a bunch of guys in pickup trucks with sirens – volunteer fire-fighters – and while they might not know completely what they were doing, at least with their strength and numbers they could do something. Back then, though, there was no 911, no phone, only Nora and Wallace and a blizzard.

I don't know what she did next. And neither does Wallace. We do know that she got him into bed, that she got him to regain consciousness, and that she saved his life. In the following days, Wallace's influenza developed into full-blown pneumonia, and this almost killed him. He stayed in bed for the better part of a month, and Nora nursed him the entire time, bathing him where he lay, bringing him steaming bowls of homemade soup, cleaning his bedpan. For the first weeks she even tried to do all the farmwork, but it was too much, and Wallace reluctantly agreed to allow her to hire a farmhand, something she had wanted to do anyway, but something that hurt his pride, for he was the third generation of Fiskes to go this land alone, and he told me that, despite his illness and his incapacity, he felt like this act had in one fell swoop made him a lesser man than either his father or his grandfather. But Nora went ahead and hired a man, remodeled the top floor of the old barn for him to live in, even piped an old woodstove through the roof so that he would have heat at night. And that made it possible for the farm to run through that winter, though it made other things possible, too, least notable of which was the damage to Wallace's pride.

6

July Fourth I spent with Kate, and we cooked steaks on the grill and ate on my porch with gin and tonics and later, when the sun was going down, we watched the lights from the fireworks in town and we listened to their gunlike reports though we could not see the fireworks themselves because of the high hills in between. It was a beautiful night, clear and warm and not too humid, and when the dark came and the two of us were sitting there alone looking at the woods, I impulsively suggested we drive to Montreal.

'Now?' Kate said.

I said, 'Right now. What is it? Two hours? I've never been. We'll get a room and stay the night. Walk the streets, have breakfast in the morning.'

'What about work? I'm supposed to be there at nine, and you have to work, too.'

'Screw work,' I said. 'We'll call in sick.'

And perhaps because this was so unlike me, because I was such a creature of routine, of habit, Kate agreed. We hastily packed an overnight bag and grabbed the gin and a bottle of tonic water and got into my Volkswagen and began to drive north.

Initially I stuck to back roads and, though I'd had more to drink than was prudent for driving, I did not care, and we rolled the windows down and the pleasant summer night came into the car and we played the radio and Kate sang along with the pop songs and I sang, too, which made her laugh. I felt in that moment freer than I had in a while, and I remember thinking that I needed to do more of this, to live in the moment, to learn how to *be*, for lack of a better word.

Eventually we reached Route 89, and soon we were at the border and the guard asked us a few questions about our intentions and length of stay and then let us through. Quickly the hilly wooded terrain of Vermont gave way to the open plains of southern Quebec, and though it was night there was a full moon and in the distance I could see groups of silos rising out of the fields like small cities. We rode through small towns with stone farmhouses right next to the highway. We rode by Catholic churches and strip clubs existing side by side. We rode by more farms and billboards in English advertising a safari adventure, which seemed out of place for this part of the world.

Kate made us drinks in plastic cups and we smoked cigarettes and for a time we had the road to ourselves and we turned off the radio and drove in silence, listening to the whirring of the tires on the two-lane highway. By the time we crossed the St Lawrence River – wide and beautiful in the dark, the lights of barges lit up like Christmas trees – it was after midnight.

We had no map, no plan, and we were entering a strange city. It took us past downtown and the tall buildings and, after going over a narrow iron trestle, I turned onto an exit ramp, and then we drove down a wide city avenue and, though it was late, the streets were full of people, walking and talking, standing in huddled groups, smoking cigarettes.

'Where to?' I said.

'Does it matter?' said Kate.

'I guess not.'

We drove until the street narrowed and the side streets were more prominent and I picked one and pulled onto it. Rue St-Denis, the sign said. I found a parking spot and parallel-parked, and we got out with our bag and began to walk.

'There is definitely a place to stay here,' I said and, sure enough, on that elegant street in the heart of Montreal's French neighborhoods, we found a small hotel that was really a renovated mansion that looked like a castle from the outside. The girl at the desk took our money and signed us in and brought us upstairs to a large, open, high-ceilinged room with a queen-size bed, a bathroom, and a balcony that looked out over the street.

I made us drinks and we went out onto the balcony. To our left I could see a busy intersection, people waiting to cross the street, cars speeding by. To our right the street and smells were like Boston but foreign, voices speaking rapidly in French rising to where we stood. I felt at once the sensory overload the city can bring and the heady mix of fear and excitement I have come to associate with it.

'Let's make love,' I said, but Kate had a different idea.

'We're in the city, let's go out.'

Farther down the same street we found a club, and outside was a group of people our age, most of them dressed in leather jackets, standing around, smoking. We moved through them and soon we were in a large and crowded room and the music was so loud I could barely hear. To our right was a dance floor and on it people were moving as if they were one solid mass, rising up with the loud bass of the song.

I shouted to Kate, 'You really want to stay here?'

'Of course,' she said. 'Get us drinks.'

'Okay,' I said and I tried to make my way to the bar, which was horseshoe-shaped and directly in front of me, but the crowd was thick so I had to angle myself between people and push a little. Soon I had managed to get close enough that I could see the bartender, a dark-haired guy in a tight, silver shirt, and I raised my hand and shouted to him that I needed two gin and tonics and he understood English well enough to make them for me.

When I turned back around to find Kate, I could not see her, and for a moment it made me nervous, that unsettling premonition that something might be wrong. But then I looked toward the dance floor and I saw her, her hands above her head, moving within the throng of dancers. For the first time I noticed her beauty in a way that others might see it, for on the dance floor she was neither a bartender nor a child of Eden; it was as if this strange city had entered into her somehow, and it dawned on me that I had never seen her move this freely, the curve of her hip beneath her jeans, her head thrown back, her mouth slightly agape, her hair swirling in front of her face. At one point she noticed me standing with the drinks and she motioned to me with her arms to come to her, but I just shook my head and mouthed the words 'no way,' and she smiled and went back to what she was doing. When the song ended she returned to me and I handed her the drink and she took a long sip and said, 'Come dance with me.'

'I can't dance,' I said.

'Sure you can, come on, Nathan.' She laughed. 'Feel the music.'

And then just as quickly as she came over she gave me back her drink to hold and returned to the floor, moving between strangers, and while I watched she sandwiched herself between a handsome Québecois couple and began to move in their small sphere, and suddenly it became intimate, the couple paying attention to her as Kate moved up toward the ceiling with her arms, the palms of her hands flattening out as she did.

Behind me some people had left the bar and I was able to find a seat. Looking back out on the floor once again, I could not find her, and then I did, and now she was dancing closely with a tall, dark man, her hands for a moment on his hips, before she dived down as if on her knees in front of him, before popping back up. It was overtly sexual, and when I saw his hands move behind her and pull her to him, I found myself torn between wanting to go push him out of the way and dragging her off to the bathroom and taking her against the sink. This was a different Kate I was watching, and I wanted her more than I ever had.

Back at the hotel, I took Kate's hand and brought her to the bed and when she kissed me I kissed her back hard on the lips and then I turned her around and undressed her while standing behind her, pulling her shirt over her head, taking her pants down while I pressed into her. She gasped when my hand shot between her legs and I could tell she was ready; and when I entered her I saw in my mind her dancing, her dropping almost to her knees in front of a strange man, and as I did I held on to her narrow shoulders and pulled her tighter onto me, and then I dropped my hands down to the small of her back and pressed there, at the spot where her belt would be if she were clothed. Later, when Kate shifted to face me, I felt her bones underneath my bones, and when I looked deep into her turquoise eyes I slowed myself down and moved patiently within her, for I saw something then I had never seen before and, without being overly sentimental about it, I want to say that what I saw was certainty, and trust, and outside, while the sounds of cars and loud voices of people leaving clubs and bars echoed, I looked into Kate's eyes and I saw myself above her, her below me, and I saw where we were joined, where we came together, where we left ourselves for something larger than both of us.

After, when we shared a cigarette, her head resting on my chest, her belly warm against my thigh, I said, 'I think I'm falling for you.'

She looked up at me, dragged on the cigarette, smiled. 'Falling?'

'Yes, falling. Falling madly in love, that's what I think.'

Kate handed the cigarette back to me, blew on the strands of blond hair that hung in front of her face so that they moved up toward me before settling back down where they were before. 'I'd say you've fallen, Nathan. Past tense.'

In the morning we slept in, waking briefly to make calls to our respective places of work, Kate to the bank, me to Connie, who laughed as if she knew I was lying to her when I said I was sick. 'No one is sick in July,' she said, but I pleaded innocence and she said she would see that a replacement was brought in to do my route.

We ate breakfast at a sidewalk café, croissants and coffee served in bowls, and we watched the people of Montreal, fashionably dressed, make their way to work, to school, wherever it was they went on a Tuesday morning. The exuberance and sheer freedom of the night before had worn off, and I was moody with a gin hangover. At one point I snapped at Kate over something silly, her wanting to see a museum, I think, and she said, 'You're a real bitch in the morning.'

After breakfast we walked around the old part of the city, looking at the architecture, at the people, and I had that sense that cities give me, where you feel significant in a paradoxical way. You would think that the countryside, with its spareness, its lack of humanity, the heightened presence of landscape, would encourage significance. But the country at times reminded me of the things that scared me, the curvature of the earth, the spinning of the planet, the unimaginable size of everything beyond the world as we know it. The city, by contrast, puts human affairs front and center and in your face, as if nothing else matters. That morning in Montreal, despite my hangover, I had that sense once again, that we were swimming like fish down crowded sidewalks, oblivious to things beyond our immediate grasp.

Later in the day we grabbed sandwiches for the ride and headed back the way we came, storm clouds threatening all through Quebec, and when we crossed the border and back into Vermont, everything instantly lovely and green, the sky opened and it began to hail, and at one point it was so heavy that the two of us pulled over on the side of the road, and in front of us we could see the red lights of other cars doing the same thing, and we sat there and watched the storm move over us, until it was gone and the sun timidly returned to the sky.

There were two messages on my answering machine when we returned to the cabin. The first was from Linger, Kate's dad, and he said he had heard that Wallace was taken to the hospital, though he did not know which one. That question was answered by the next message, which was from a nurse at Fletcher Allen, who said Wallace Fiske had suffered a heart attack but was expected to make a full recovery. She said he had listed me as his next of kin and could really use his friend, which touched me, because it seemed so vulnerable for Wallace to request something like that, to refer to me that way, and though I was very worried about him, I drove to the hospital buoyed by the fact that he needed me, and that I could be of service.

WALLACE WAS on the third floor, in a private room, which surprised me, and he had been taken out of intensive care the night before. Apparently, he had collapsed while chopping wood, and he was next to the road so that some guy driving by had seen him and stopped and realized it was his heart and called the ambulance. Wallace was conscious the whole time, though in a great deal of pain, and when they got him to the hospital they were able to perform an emergency angioplasty, which did the trick, at least to the doctor's satisfaction.

I opened the door to his room slowly, not sure what to expect, and when I saw him I felt something give inside me, for he was lying on the bed with his eyes half-closed, his head propped up, an intravenous needle stuck into the left arm. His normally ruddy complexion was an off shade of gray and, while he did not look particularly ill other than that, it was odd to see him, this man of the outdoors, this farmer, in a hospital bed, chained to it by the long tube of the intravenous. I thought immediately of the squirrel in the cage trap.

I stepped in. 'Wallace,' I said, almost a whisper.

His eyes opened, and he saw me there. 'Where is it?'

I looked at him. 'What?'

'The scotch, dammit.'

'I didn't know you wanted scotch.'

Wallace sighed. 'They didn't give you the message?'

'The nurse said you needed your friend,' I said, and then I got it. His friend was the scotch. It figured.

'Exactly,' Wallace said.

'Sorry, I didn't realize that's what you meant. I'm not sure they want you drinking in here anyway.'

'I'm seventy-nine years old. I don't give a shit what they want. What do you say, Nathan? There's money in the coat.'

He raised his hand to where his Carhartt jacket sat slung over a chair.

Around the corner from the hospital I found a state liquor store, and I bought a bottle of Highland scotch. Once outside I tucked it into my pants and pulled my shirt over it, shielding it with my arm. Smuggling a bottle of scotch into a hospital, I thought. If it wasn't silly, it would probably be funny.

Back in his room, I opened the scotch for him and handed him the bottle. With his free arm he brought it to his lips and sipped hard, and I helped him take it back down so that it would not spill. He repeated this gesture, and I helped him once again, and this time he had me cap it and I slid the bottle under the sheet covering his legs.

'That's better,' he said.

'How are you feeling?'

'Ah, you know. As good as can be expected. It didn't kill me.'

'Did they say how long you'd be here?'

'Another day, maybe two. I'd like to go now, but they won't let me.'

'Is there anything I can do? The cows?'

'Nah. The cows will be fine. They can stay out in the field until I get back. In this weather it won't hurt them. But the dog, that would help – can you feed the dog?'

I said, 'Sure.'

'Thanks, Nathan.' He looked over toward the window and I followed his eyes, through the curtains to the sunlit day, a slice of building from the other side of the hospital, the outer reaches of the parking lots. I suddenly had the urge to get out

of here, to be back in Eden, where the greenness of everything made the idea of illness seem impossible, distant. For
some reason I thought of a documentary I had seen on the
nature channel a few weeks back. It followed herds of wilde-
beest as they migrated across the Serengeti Plain. As they
went, members of the herd were picked off by predators, lions
and packs of wild dogs; they drowned by the dozens in swollen
rivers; and some simply succumbed to the overwhelming heat,
falling onto the parched earth, their flanks heaving before stopping altogether, the camera lingering for a moment before
moving on. It struck me when I saw it that humanity has such
an assumption of life, when in fact the opposite is true. We
are too often surprised by tragedy, or that fateful call, like the
one I received telling me of my father's death. In truth, I figure
we should be surprised that we manage to make it through
the day, to wake to see another morning.

When I left the hospital, it was early evening, but the sun
was still high in the sky. Rounding a bend before the town
center of Eden, I was suddenly driving right toward the bright
summer sun and, for an instant, everything was gold, shiny,
shimmering gold, gold trees, gold sky, gold world.

7

It was when Wallace returned from the hospital, a few days later, that he first mentioned the name Guy LaRoche. He was on doctor's orders to stay in bed, and he did, as he had forty years before, after almost freezing in the snow behind the house.

While Wallace remained in the hospital, I had been dutifully coming over to feed the dog. To do so, I had to venture into Wallace's basement, where he kept several thirty-gallon bags full of Ide's dog food. It was an old Vermont farmhouse basement, low-ceilinged, earthen-floored, with a thick, partially rotted sill that made its way above a makeshift foundation. Since Wallace had no electricity, the place was devoid of wires, and the only piping came out of an antique cistern in one corner that was fed by a well. In the middle of the basement there was a pile of loose slate and granite that almost reached the ceiling, as if when the basement was dug they decided simply to leave this behind. It was dark even in midday, though once your eyes adjusted you could see adequately because the bulk-head that led to the outside was cracked and falling apart, and slivers of sunlight came through to the ground. It was in that basement that I found only the second photograph of Wallace's I had ever seen.

It was nailed to the sill, up against the ceiling, and I saw it while I was exploring around, looking at the old farm tools Wallace had stacked here and there, the bags of lime and agricultural chemicals that seemed to be strewn everywhere. I reached up and took it down and looked at it. It showed two men in the pasture behind Wallace's house, the old barn visible behind them, and I could tell it was summer by the height of the marshy grass growing next to the road. Each man held the reins of a horse in his hands, the horses standing behind them, one giant and big-headed, mottled white in color, the other a slender, brown Morgan.

This time I recognized Wallace right away, thin and tall, his angular face, and he had the white horse, a pair of overalls on, no shirt underneath, his arms sinewy and muscular. Next to him was a smaller man with wavy, dark hair, small, almost serpentine dark eyes, a flat nose, and high cheekbones. He wore a brown suit that looked too small for him, so that you could see where his bare arms protruded out of the sleeves, and underneath it he wore a white collarless shirt, which also was too small, and on his feet he had knobby boots that looked much too big. Despite the awkwardness of his clothes, however, there was something about him that struck me, an intensity, a handsomeness, perhaps, and he seemed to possess a coiled strength that you sometimes see in small, wiry men.

I took the photograph upstairs with me, which I should not have done, but I wanted to see it better, in the light. Then for some inexplicable reason, perhaps because I liked the picture so much, I slid it into the breast pocket of my shirt, where I kept it until Wallace returned from the hospital.

They reluctantly released Wallace early, the doctor telling me that he really needed more time but that he was such – and this is honestly what the doctor, a nice, gray-bearded man, said – a pain in the ass, that they thought they might as well let him convalesce at home as long as I was willing to help out and keep him from doing farmwork, which I was more or less able to do.

It was while I was helping out, bringing his lunch to where he lay in the upstairs bedroom, wistfully looking out the window to Mirror Lake below, that I took out the photograph and handed it to him.

'I found this in the basement,' I said.

Wallace took it from my hand and his bloodshot eyes went to it for only an instant before he handed it back to me. 'Put it back,' he said.

'I'm sorry,' I said. 'I didn't think it was a big deal.'

Wallace sighed. 'It's okay. Laying in this bed makes me think of Guy enough as it is.'

'Guy?'

'Yes, Guy LaRoche. The man with me in the picture.'

'Guy,' I said, saying it again, liking the way it sounded,

different from how it was spelled, rhyming with *key*. 'French,'
I said.

'French Canadian,' said Wallace, 'Québecois.'

And so as we were sitting in Wallace's bedroom, his lunch
of grilled cheese and ham growing cold, he began to tell me
about Guy. It was during Wallace's bout with pneumonia that
Nora got him to grudgingly agree to hire a man to help out
with the farm. Apparently, this was not as easy as it sounds.
In 1950 there was hardly an excess of unemployed young men
in Eden, some having been killed in the war in Europe and
the Pacific, some currently fighting on the Korean peninsula,
others moving west or to the cities in search of greater oppor-
tunity. Those that were young, like Wallace, owned their own
farms and had plenty of work to do. Nonetheless, Nora put
the word out through the normal channels, other farmers
mainly, and through the church and the general store. A week
passed and she heard nothing. Then one day – during a winter
thaw at the end of that January, when the temperature soared
into the sixties, and the sun shone hot, snow melting off the
roof, the roads quickly becoming mud – Nora was coming out
of the barn when she saw a man walking up the road.

Wallace saw him, too, from essentially where he lay while
telling me this story, the barking of the dogs causing him to
look out. He was a sight. His clothes were makeshift and torn,
and even from a distance you could tell he needed a bath. He
carried a bag over his shoulder and a walking stick in the other
hand, which from the looks of it was half used to prop him
up, since he was pale and gaunt and looked frail.

Nora met him on the road, and they had a conversation,

and within minutes Wallace saw her leading him to the barn. She took him up to the loft, where she showed him the room she had put together, the simple metal bed and mattress, an old wooden bureau, a woodstove on top of cinder blocks, its piping jury-rigged through a small hole in the roof. She left him there to start a fire while she returned to the house.

Upstairs she told Wallace what she knew. His name was Guy LaRoche, he was from northern Quebec, and he had heard at the general store that they had work.

'What does he know about a farm?' Wallace asked.

'He said he grew up on one, knew his way around.'

Nora brought Guy to the house and fed him, then brought him upstairs to meet Wallace. Wallace looked him over. He was a mess, it was true, his neck and hands caked with dirt, and his eyes and his voice and his posture suggesting years of hard living. But there was something about him as well, a strength, that Wallace saw, and when they spoke they spoke in generalities about farmwork, about expectations. Wallace did not ask him where he had been, or where he came from, or what his story was, for that was Wallace's way then, as it always was: let a man tell his story at the time he feels is right, not when you want to know it. Instead, Wallace asked him if he knew how to milk, which he did, if he knew about horses, about pigs, about sugaring, about crops. Guy said he knew all those things with the exception of sugaring, which he had never done but figured he could learn as he went. It's easy, Wallace told him, that may be the easiest thing we do. Then he said: I think you'll like it here on Mirror Lake.

In the days that followed Guy found his way around the

hill farm, and from his room upstairs Wallace saw the confidence with which he handled himself, his way with the animals, the horses especially, and through the floorboards of the old house he could hear Nora preparing Guy meals and then the two of them sitting down together. Though he could not hear their conversation, he knew they were talking, and sometimes the sounds of her laughter drifted up to him and he smiled. He liked to hear her laugh.

At night, while he ate in bed, Nora briefed him on the farm, on Guy, on what got done, when the milk truck was coming, what projects they worked on.

'He's a good worker, Wallace,' Nora said.

'Get him a bath yet?' Wallace asked, smiling.

'That he could still use.'

One snowy afternoon about two weeks into Guy's stay, Wallace was lying in bed, looking out the window, watching the snow fall onto the ice-covered lake, when there was a knock at the door. 'Come in,' he said, and it opened and Guy stood there. He nodded to Wallace and looked down at his feet.

'What is it?' Wallace said.

'Sorry to bother you,' said Guy, 'but I could really use some clothes.'

Wallace looked him over, at his shoes with visible holes, the worn pants, the wool jacket with the slit almost fully exposing his right shoulder. 'Tell Nora to get you some of my old stuff. She knows where it is.'

Later, Wallace was lying in bed and he felt stronger, he had not slept all afternoon, and he could hear Nora and Guy at the dinner table. He decided to rise, and when he stood he realized how weak his legs were, his calf muscles almost atrophied, but he steadied himself and made his way to the door. He opened the door and stepped on the stairs, half-expecting Nora to call out to him, but she did not, and he made his way slowly down until he could look around the corner of the stairwell to the kitchen, where they sat in the glow of an oil lamp. In front of them on the table were an open can of sardines, some bread, a jar of pickles from last summer. Guy had a glass of whiskey, and he now had on some of Wallace's clothes, a white shirt he had outgrown, a pair of wool pants. Nora had her back to Wallace, but he could see the way she leaned toward Guy, her elbows on the table, and together they talked softly, too softly for Wallace to pick up the words.

He felt in that moment as if he were looking through a window into someone else's life, as if he were watching another married couple at their farm table, breaking bread, sharing conversation. He stood in silence and watched them, the way children sneak down the stairs when their parents have guests and spy on the unsuspecting adults. Guy had cleaned up, and the dirt that had seemed permanently caked onto his neck and face was gone, in its place freshly scrubbed pink skin. He had also shaved, and he looked like a different man from the one that had walked up the road a few weeks back. His face had filled out, his hair was pushed neatly back away from his forehead, his narrow, dark eyes no longer hidden under a sunken brow.

Wallace was about to take another step and then he decided not to. He decided to stand there, on the steps, taking them in. He watched them talk, he watched their rapport, so natural, and he took in his living room, his kitchen, his house. He had been in bed so long he saw it with new eyes. He stayed motionless until Nora rose to bring some dishes toward the sink, and he saw her fully, her beauty, her curly hair down against the back of her neck. In that moment he realized he had grown too comfortable with her, and it took seeing her in the company of another man to make him understand that.

WITHIN A few weeks Wallace began to feel stronger, and to spend more time out of his room. At first he merely moved downstairs, substituting a rocking chair in front of the woodstove for his bed. From there he watched the snow fall through the window, watched it continue to pile as it had all winter long, sticking to the spindly branches of the large maples that lined the road down toward the pond. Soon, though, he felt good enough to be back at work, and he started slowly, waking to milk with Guy, taking pleasure in the simple things he had always done, the cool air in his lungs in the winter morning, the feel of the teat between his fingers, the squeeze and pull that he had been doing since he was old enough to walk, the sight of the creamy white milk against the gray of the pail between his legs.

Wallace saw that Guy was a good worker, steady and competent, and the two of them labored in silence those first mornings, getting the feel of each other, and for Wallace it was odd at first to have another man in the fields with him, it had not been that way since his father died, but he found that he liked it, someone beyond Nora to share the experience with, to understand the subtle comfort he derived from tangible hard work.

In early March they began to cut next year's wood, spending all day in the woodlot on the hill high above the lake. They used a team of horses and a skidder, and the snowpack was deep with a hard crust so they left the team out in the meadow while they chopped down large ash trees, removing the limbs and then turning the trunks into manageable-size logs. Then the two of them would hook the logs onto the skidder with fifty feet of chain and the horses would pull them out. They did this over and over until the logs piled in the meadow equaled fifteen cords. It was arduous work, and when they went at it, they went at it hard, though there were times when they took a break, sitting down on the pile to smoke, to watch the blue late winter sky, the iced-over lake gray below them.

It was then, sitting on the wood, their breath and smoke filling the air, the large horses eating out of feed bags, mist rising off their nostrils, that Wallace and Guy became something resembling friends. At first their conversations were limited to the chores at hand, what was next, speculation on how many more of the large ash they would need to take down to reach their goal. But gradually they began to move on to other things, and one afternoon when a light snow fell on them through a sky of clouds and sun, Guy told Wallace about his past.

Guy said he had grown up on a large dairy farm in northern Quebec, on land that − unlike southern Quebec, which was plains and prairie − was similar to this part of Vermont, mountainous and wooded, with lakes, streams, rivers. A land of rocky soil, fit for not much more than cows. He was one of five boys, and the youngest, so that when his father died when Guy was only sixteen, the rules of primogeniture they practiced dictated that his oldest brother inherited everything. Guy's mother was still alive, and he was welcome to stay on the farm as a hand, but he decided that he wanted something else, though he did not know what. He left for Montreal, where he found work in a factory that made wooden furniture, and it was good, honest labor and he was skilled at it. The owner of the factory, a man named Potvin, put him up in an apartment in town, and he was young and had some money in his pocket and the city was an exciting place to be.

But things changed when Guy fell in love. Her name was Michelle and she was pretty and nice but she was also Potvin's daughter, who saw Guy as a hard worker but someone who was beneath her in class. Michelle told Guy this and he shrugged it off, but often when they were together, lying on the cot in his one-room apartment, she would bring it up, let him know how important it was that her father not find out about them. And, for six months or so, they were successful.

Then, one morning, as Michelle was leaving Guy's apartment, she opened the door and her father filled the frame. He was a big man, heavyset, with a jowly face, a prominent nose, and a thick, gray mustache. He immediately pushed her back into the room, where Guy still lay in bed, and when Guy rose up he saw Potvin slap his daughter across the face with a force that made tears run down her cheeks. Guy went quickly to him and pushed him against the door, but the larger man slammed his weight into Guy and drove him into the wall, taking him by the throat. If you ever see my daughter again, he said, I will kill you.

After Potvin and Michelle had left, Guy gathered his few belongings and was back out on the street. He checked into a motel and for weeks tried to make contact with Michelle, waiting in the shadows at night outside the row house where she lived with her father. In the mornings he was there as well, and one day after her father left the house he noticed that she did not come out with him, and he waited a few minutes before he made his way to the door. When he knocked on the door he saw the curtain part on an upstairs window, and he caught a glimpse of the woman he loved, her dark hair, her eyes, and he knocked again though she did not answer. He began to knock frantically, pounding on the door, saying 'I love you' over and over. Finally the door opened a crack, and he saw the chain first and then Michelle and she said, 'You must leave.'

He pleaded his love and he saw that her eyes were wet, but she said, 'I don't love you, Guy. And I never want to see you again.'

He made her repeat it and she did and when he asked for a third time, certain she could not do it, she started to and then stopped, closing the door quickly. Guy heard her weeping behind the large wooden door, but he stopped knocking. Finally, he told her through the door where he was staying and asked her to meet him there later that afternoon.

In the motel room Guy waited quietly, sitting on the edge of the bed, his hands locked around his knees, rocking slightly back and forth. On the desk next to the small bed the clock ticked off each minute. And still no Michelle. He was about to give up when he heard footfalls in the hallway and he perked up, stood, and went to the door. When he opened it, they were on him.

Three men plus Potvin, who sat in a chair and watched while they worked him over, punching him in the stomach and head until he crumpled to the ground and then taking turns kicking him. Guy thought he would die. He remembered the feel of the shod boot against his kidneys – like a finger into a balloon – before he passed out.

Guy came to in an alley behind the motel, surrounded by rotting trash. He did not know how long he had been out. He knew his ribs were broken and perhaps his leg, for he could not stand. It hurt to breathe. For two days he slept on the street. On the third day he was strong enough to move, and he began to walk, aware of how he must have looked, bruised and battered, a pronounced limp, uncertain of where he was going, but knowing that he needed to get out of the city. He walked for a week, begging food along the way, eating in small farmhouses' kitchens, sleeping under the summer stars at night. Eventually Guy found himself at the door of a large farm near Saint Fortunat, and the elderly farm couple took him in, gave him a room, and for two years he worked as their farmhand. Then in rapid succession they died, the old man of a stroke, his wife two days later of a broken heart. The bank seized the farm for past debts, and once again Guy was on the road. He drifted south from place to place, finally crossing the border and making his way to Eden in the dead of winter because he liked the name when he first saw it on a sign. At the general store they told him about work at the Fiske house, and that is how he came to live with Wallace and Nora.

When he finished his story, Wallace lit another cigarette and looked out to where smoke from the chimney on his house rose above the tree line. 'That's some story,' he said.

'Yes,' said Guy.

'The woman, Michelle?'

'Yes.'

'You never saw her again?'

'No.'

'Do you think about her?'

'I try not to, but sometimes I can't help it.'

Wallace drew on his cigarette, thought about that. 'We need to find you a wife,' he said, and he smiled.

Guy smiled back and stood, ready to return to work. He said, 'Something tells me Eden isn't the place for that.'

'Well, you never know,' Wallace said. 'I did all right.'

'Yes, you did. You did better than all right,' Guy said, and then the two men returned to the woodlot, to the grove of tall ash, to their silence.

8

August in Eden is one of those transition months, still summer but almost fall, the days perceptibly shorter, the air cooler at night, the deep, lush green present but somehow muted. While the rest of the country is deep in the throes of summer, Vermonters know that in a few short weeks the first leaves will begin to change, the first frost will coat the grass in the morning, the short growing season coming to an end, the heady promise of summer giving way to the slow decline of fall.

August, as well, was a transition month for Kate and me. I had fallen for her completely, the romantic love of our early time together starting to take root, to blossom into something altogether different. In a way this was what I did not think I was capable of, and it would have made me happy if it were not for one clear reality: Kate seemed oblivious to it all. She shook off my entreaties of a more profound love the way she shook off everything. It was as if I was simply something else she did with her day, like her job at the bank, her occasional filling in at the bar, a brisk walk down one of the dirt roads of Eden. At the same time it frustrated me, I also found it rather intoxicating, and I made it my personal mission to make her love me more.

She'd come over for dinner and I'd meet her at the door, leaning against the wall seductively, and when she'd say, 'What are you doing?' I'd shush her, go to her, take her in my arms, lead her to bed. She liked this new me, the impulsive me, the one who would quickly suggest going to Montreal, who would show up at the bank in the middle of the day with a handmade love note, a single rose. She liked it but, at the same time, she seemed remarkably unimpressed. The more unimpressed she was, the more I tried.

One night I told her I wanted to walk after dinner, and the two of us began a slow amble down the dirt road from my cabin. The sun had just set and the August evening was mildly cool, the sky a beautiful mix of purples and reds over the mountain. We walked arm in arm, the woods around us, the hard dirt road beneath our feet, the song of birds in the trees, the distant sounds of cars out on the main road. At a parting in the trees where you could see clear across the valleys of Eden to the other highlands, to the mountains, nothing but trees in between, no houses visible, we stopped and I turned toward the view and separated myself from her arm.

'What is it?' she said.

'I thought I saw something.'

'Where?'

'Over there, near the trees.'

'It's nothing,' she said, turning to keep going down the road.

'Wait,' I said, and I went toward the edge of the road, toward the sharp drop-off, the gulch below me, the trees moving downhill away from me. I reached behind a large oak where I had earlier hidden the bottle of champagne, two plastic flutes, a bar of Swiss chocolate, a pint of fresh strawberries.

'Nathan,' Kate said.

'It looks like someone left these here.'

She came over to see what I was talking about. For a minute I had her, and then she saw the bottle of champagne in my hand and smiled, and we sat right there on the lip of the road, our feet dangling over the side where the forest wall fell away, watching the remnants of the sun in the sky above Camels Hump. We drank champagne out of the flutes and ate chocolate and strawberries and Kate said, 'This is nice.'

'I hope whoever left these here doesn't come looking for them,' I said.

'Nathan Carter,' she said, leaning over to kiss me, 'you are a bad liar.'

Later, back at the house, we made love in a chair on the porch, the cool air all around us, stars out, the night crisp and beautiful. When we were finished I was full of love talk, and she laughed at me when I told her how I would hold her all night, how I would fill her with so much love she would not know what to do with it, how it would fill the entire back of her pickup truck so that it might tip over on the way home, and then, when she made it home, she would wake to discover that the land around the house she shared with Linger would be full of roses, tulips, all kinds of flowers, birds, sunshine, and all other kinds of good things.

I said, 'Then when you're not here, I'll miss you like I miss June in January.'

'It's August.'

'You know what I mean.'

'You're drunk,' she said.

'I'm sorry.'

'Don't be, I like it.'

In this way Kate and I continued our push and pull, my push closer to her, her commonsense reaction. It was physics at its most basic.

In the second week of August, summer suddenly came roaring back with an intensity we had not seen in my time here. It was an old-fashioned heat wave, every day in the high nineties, high humidity, thick, oppressive air. My postal Jeep had no air-conditioning, and I drove with the windows down, the hot sun beating on the dashboard, sweat soaking my hair by midmorning. When I reached Mirror Lake I'd stop and say a quick hello to Wallace – who was back to his old self, oblivious to the heat, working, remarkably, in a flannel shirt and jeans – and then quickly head to the shore of the lake, peel my clothes off down to my boxer shorts, and dive into the cool water, floating out on my back, diving under for more coolness. It seemed the only relief on days like that, and at night I'd do it again, meeting Kate after work, and the two of us would swim out into the middle of the lake, treading water until we grew tired, then heading back in and drying off until we were hot again, and then returning to the water. Despite the heat, it was a beautiful time, and I had Kate to myself and we were young and it was summer and I do not know what else you can ask for in this life.

THEN, JUST as quickly as the heat wave hit, something for the first time came between Kate and me. I had always known that she had boyfriends before I came along, though I chose not to ask about it, and when she made subtle references to a Steve or a Kevin, I did not probe. And, unlike me, she had little need to talk about past relationships and, when I think about it now, I realize how much of a double standard I practiced in this regard, for I was always relating experiences about women I'd been with, what we had done together, how it had ended. She listened patiently, and seemed genuinely curious, and was not at all threatened by my past, something I now understand was indicative of her strength.

One afternoon I was on the last leg of my route, driving through Gospel Hollow, coming down that long hill into the valley where the church stands alone framed by green hills, when I saw Kate's brown pickup pull out of a side road in the distance ahead. It quickly rounded the bend by the brook and, though it was not the way my route led, I decided to follow, curious that she was not at work. When I turned the corner, I did not see her, because the road meandered like the brook below, rocky land all around, cows down by the brook, grazing in twos and threes. I picked her up around the next turn, just before she hit the straightaway, and I saw two heads.

I followed at a safe distance so she could not see me, and

she led me up Frazier Road and into the hinterlands of Eden, a part I did not know well, past large farms with open, rolling hills and views of the mountains. The road then dipped down into the woods again, and here there were trailers tucked into the forest, narrow dirt driveways leading to them. We drove until I saw her turn into a driveway on the left, and when I reached it I saw the driveway bend back into the woods, and the house or trailer back there was not visible from the road. I pulled over to the side and got out.

Slowly I began to walk down the driveway. I heard the sound of the pickup truck doors closing and, when I made it to where the driveway curved, I saw the house, a log cabin, set back in the small clearing, and then I saw Kate, on the porch with a man about my age with curly hair and a thin beard. They were sitting in rocking chairs and were passing a joint back and forth. I heard Kate's laughter, and at one point I saw her put her hand on his shoulder. What was this? What was I watching? Was she cheating on me? Was that possible?

I stood silently for about ten minutes, watching them, feeling the anger rise like boiling water inside me. Then I walked back to my car and stayed there for another ten minutes, too, chain-smoking cigarettes, my heart racing with adrenaline. I wondered if I should confront her now, but that was not my way, so I returned to finish my route, trying to ignore the feeling of devastation I had, a creeping dread that I felt I could beat back by trying not to think about it.

After work I drove to Kate's house and her truck was not there. The afternoon was muggy and thunderclouds gathered over the mountains, but overhead the sun was still bright and the sky cloudless. I parked in the dirt driveway in front of the bar, which did not open for another hour, and I turned off my engine and waited. Shortly I saw Linger coming down the outdoor staircase from their apartment, and he waved when he saw me and came over to the window of my car. He had a cigarette in his mouth, and he made a motion with his hand of lighting a lighter and I pulled mine out of the breast pocket of my shirt and lit his dangling cigarette for him.

'Hello, Linger,' I said.

'Kate's not here.'

'I know.'

He nodded, dragged on his smoke. 'Looks like some boomers coming our way,' he said, motioning toward the mountains, where the clouds were black and ominous-looking. As he did I saw a crack of lightning snap in the sky.

'Indeed. Do you know where Kate is?'

'No, I haven't seen her since this morning. Assume she's still working.'

'Yeah, must be. Well, tell her I stopped by, okay?'

'You bet,' Linger said, dropping his cigarette on the dirt, turning his back to me. I watched as he unlocked the bar and disappeared inside, and then I drove home, the storm moving overhead right before I reached my road, the rain falling hard, the thunder still off in the distance, a deep and low rumbling in the sky.

I WAS inside making dinner about six when Kate called. It was still raining, though the thunderstorms – intense and furious – had already moved through. Out the window I could see mist rising in the yard.

'Hey,' she said.

I wasted no time. 'Did you break my heart?'

'What are you talking about?'

'Did you break my heart?'

'Nathan, I don't know what that means. What's wrong with you?'

'I saw you today.'

'You did?'

'Yes.'

'Where?'

'You tell me.'

'Nathan, I'm not going to play games. Where did you see me?'

'Who is he?'

'Who is who?'

'The guy with you in the car. The guy with the house in the woods.'

'You followed me?'

'Yes, Kate, I did.'

She paused. 'I don't believe this.'

'That was precisely my reaction.'

'What, are you stalking me?'

'No. I saw you with another man and I was curious. You would have done the same thing.'

'That's where you are wrong, Nathan.'

'Are you sleeping with him?'

'I'm not going to answer that.'

'Just tell me. I'd rather hear it from you.'

'This conversation is over,' Kate said, and then she hung up.

After that, I went outside and smoked a cigarette. The rain had stopped but there were puddles on the porch and the air was sweet with water. Low-hanging clouds moved like apparitions above the hills. Mist hung in the valley below the cabin, giving the illusion that I was at a higher altitude than I was, as if I were on some peak in the Andes. The humidity had lifted, and the early evening was pleasant, not quite cool, but a light breeze.

When I reached Kate's house some fifteen minutes later, the bar was open and I could see through the plate-glass windows that there were a few patrons in early, Linger behind the counter, the Red Sox game on the television. I went up the outdoor staircase to the apartment and stood for a moment before I knocked. Through the door I could see the glow of the television in the living room, and somewhere in the back a light was on, though the kitchen in front of me was dark. I rapped my knuckles against the small window on the door and then did it again. Kate emerged from the shadows and opened the door.

'What do you want?'

'To talk.'

She crossed her arms over her chest, looked at me. 'About?'

'Come on, Kate, cut me a break.'

She looked at me long and hard, as if she was thinking about it. 'Okay,' she said, 'Let's go for a ride.'

We drove the back way to Mirror Lake, on the winding dirt

road that took us up and over Lane Hill, the road that culmi-
nated in that dangerous grade with the hairpin turn, the turn
I'd failed to make that first December, the one that had landed
me in Wallace's spare room. We drove in silence, Kate as far
away from me as she could be in the front seat of the postal
Jeep, leaning against the left-side door, while I drove on the
right. When I started down the large hill before Wallace's
house, I put the Jeep in first like I always did, the engine noise
rising high as it braked against gravity itself, and we took the
turn smoothly, Wallace's fields, and then his house, and then
the lake opening up before us. There was one lamp lit in
Wallace's house, and I knew he was in his chair next to the
stove, probably sitting in the half-dark with his pipe and his
scotch. We rode the small hill down, and now the lake was
on our left, smooth and black and calm in the cloudy dark.

I parked on the opposite shore from Wallace's house, pulling
the Jeep into the tall grass that lined the road. Kate was out
first and I followed, and she sat on the hood and dangled her
legs and I climbed up next to her and we lit cigarettes and
listened to the lake sounds, the cry of a loon, the slap of a
trout against the surface, the music of crickets in the tall grass.

I spoke first. I said, 'I'm sorry I followed you.'

'You should be.'

'It was wrong.'

'Yes, it was.'

I looked at her, her profile, the clean lines of her face. 'What
about what you did?'

'What? Spend time with an old friend? Since when is that
a crime?'

'Is that what he is? An old friend?'

'Yes, Nathan, Jesus. I mean, what do you think? I'm fucking someone else?'

'In the absence of other information, perhaps.'

Kate turned toward me and I saw the anger in her eyes. 'Your insecurity is embarrassing.'

'It's not insecurity,' I said.

'No, you're right,' she said. 'It's lack of trust. Which is worse.'

'I trust you, Kate,' I said, knowing that it sounded hollow as I said it.

'Then show me,' she said, throwing her cigarette out into the wet grass. 'Give me a reason to believe you.'

ONCE YOU open that door and allow jealousy to come between you, it is very difficult simply to close it back up. It lingers like a cold, eating away at the two of you, and something has to give. Kate and I went on after that, pretty much as we did before, but we both knew that things had changed, that a shift had occurred. The man I saw her with was her friend, someone she grew up with who had recently moved back to Eden. His name was Sam, and he bears little relevance to this story other than what I have told you so far.

In the weeks that followed my first sighting of them together, Kate spent more and more time with him, and when I brought it up with her she grew quickly angry as if it were beyond my right to ask about what she did, when she did it, and with whom. One time she even told me that I was 'going to lose her' if I did not let it go, and that worked for a short period, at least I tried to make it work, though it was difficult, for my mind has a tendency to leap to conclusions, and in this case I found myself constantly imagining her within his embrace, the two of them in bed together, he inside her. It was not healthy and it drove me crazy, always wondering what she was doing when she was not with me, and she made it worse for she did not invite me into her time with Sam. She kept the two of us separate, and this only served to heighten my anxiety.

A few days before Labor Day, I was explaining this to Wallace as I helped him move an astonishing number of wooden doors out of his barn and into the basement so he could make more room for his chickens. The doors were stacked on top of one another, and were old and heavy, but Wallace, a month removed from a heart attack, held up his end fine, and I did my best, carrying them one at a time to the house across the expanse of pasture. The day was warm with a mottled blue sky, the sun moving in and out of high clouds. We worked steadily for an hour, then stopped and sat on the porch, sipping iced tea.

'You should back off,' Wallace said.

'What do you mean?'

'With Kate.'

'Yeah, I guess.'

'Give her the space she needs. Or you will lose her.'

'It's hard.'

'I know it, but you got no choice. Trust me on this one.'

And I did, took Wallace's advice, told Kate that she had nothing to worry about from me. That I would never ask her again about Sam or get in the way of her seeing him or anyone else, as long as I got my time with her, too. This required that I bury within myself the feelings I had, put them away some-where, swallow them like bad-tasting medicine. And, for the most part, I succeeded. Heading into the fall, Kate and I had an uneasy peace, a love that may have stalled but refused to quit. In early September the leaves started to change, slowly, a hint of red here, a splash of yellow there. Soon the hills would be filled with radiant color. I never really thought about it before I came to Eden. But, as beautiful as the colors are, they are also a harbinger of something deeper and darker, soon to be bare branches, life in hibernation, subtle enough to be easily confused with death.

9

That first year Guy was on the farm, spring came too fast for such a deep and long winter. Mirror Lake overflowed its shores, and the tiny brooks and streams that flowed in and out of it turned into turbulent rivers. Out in the pastures the water pooled as high as Wallace's waist. The quick thaw turned the roads into impassable mud bogs, and for two weeks the milk truck could not make its run. One afternoon a calf wandered away from the high fields and found itself stuck in one of the newly formed rivers, the water churning around its narrow legs, a tree branch keeping the animal from being swept away, its childlike baying audible up at the house. Wallace waded into the water with a rope around him, Guy holding the other end of it, and he made it through the strong current to rescue the calf.

In time, though, the water receded, the earth began to

harden, and the busiest season on the farm began. Fields were plowed, manure laid, corn and rye planted, a new chicken coop was built, the barn and house were repainted. Pigs and chickens were slaughtered and driven to the train station in Saint Johnsbury, where they were shipped to markets south to be sold. The kitchen garden was tilled, and Nora planted tomatoes, peppers, onions, fresh herbs, potatoes, carrots, and celery. The first flowers shot through the dirt, and the rosebushes in the front yard bloomed. A cat birthed a litter in the barn below Guy's room. Wallace shot a sick fisher in the grove of trees behind the chicken coop. And on a beautiful day in the middle of May, after Wallace had caught three trout from the lake's edge, Nora told him she was with child.

They were on the porch, Nora sitting in a rocking chair while Wallace sat on the steps, a tin pail between his legs, cleaning the fish.

She said, 'I have some news.'

He looked up at her, the knife in his hands, its blade about to disembowel the silvery rainbow trout. 'Oh?'

'I'm pregnant.'

Wallace looked down for a second, put the trout into the bucket, placed the knife on the porch step, wiped his hands clean with a cloth, and stood and went to her. He smiled wide and picked her up out of the chair and held her in his arms, smelled her hair, and said to her, 'This is great.'

'It's early,' Nora said.

'Are you sure then?'

'I think so. I've been spotting for a week.'

'My God,' he said, 'I thought maybe, you know –'

'No,' she said, 'you can.'

Wallace held her away from him then, his hands on her arms, looked her in the eyes, and said something he had not said to her since the day they were wed. He said, 'I love you.'

'I know,' Nora said.

Wallace had always thought when he got married that he would have children. It seemed a foregone conclusion. It was the way things were. You got married, and children soon followed. Someone to carry on with the farm after he had gone, like he had done for his father, and his father for his father. There was a simple symmetry to that idea, old as Eden itself. He secretly hoped for a boy, for he knew a boy was more likely to stay on the farm, though he did not rule out the fact that a girl could just as well take over.

He surprised himself, though, with the depth of the feeling he had when Nora told him. On the one hand, Wallace had resigned himself to the fact that, as he said, he might not have one in the chamber. Now that he knew that was not true, he was awash with feeling – pride, hope, anxiety. And the love he had for Nora was rekindled in a way that reminded him that perhaps it had diminished some over time. Not that it had disappeared, but seeing her in a new light with something they shared growing within her, a big-eyed baby, an amalgamation of both their histories, made Wallace want to give more of himself to her, to treat her the way he had when they first met, sitting on a log on a warm evening with their feet dangling over the lake, the fading sun setting in its black reflection. But he knew, as well, that there was no going back. There was only forward, and that was enough.

That night they celebrated by having dinner with Guy, the three of them eating the trout with fresh butter and herbs and Guy and Wallace raising glasses of whiskey. Nora retired early and Wallace stayed up late into the night, drinking too much, smoking with his friend, his farmhand, feeling warm and generous about the world. When he finally joined Nora in bed, she was asleep with her back to him, and he climbed in bed and spooned with her, his arms wrapping around her, his hands placed firmly on the slight round of her belly.

IN THE mornings she was sick and Wallace's heart went out to her as he rose to do the milking, hearing her in the small room off the kitchen, throwing up into the basin. But he knew she was strong, and she was, shaking off the sickness for what it was: something that could not be avoided, a means to an end. In the evenings she was more tired than usual, and took to the couch after dinner while Wallace shared a drink and a smoke with Guy on the porch. By the time he returned Nora would be fast asleep, and he would gently wake her and help her up the stairs to the bed.

By June she was starting to show, not much, but enough for the baby to become more obvious to Wallace's eye, a visible mass, sitting low, below her navel. One afternoon the midwife visited, and Wallace was in the fields with Guy, moving the cows to a new pasture, and he saw her leave, a slight crone of a woman, and later when he returned to the house Nora was out in the garden, weeding on her knees, and the sun was hot and Wallace said, 'Think you should be doing that?' suddenly protective over her, but she smiled at him as if to say, 'Leave it alone.'

Nora put down her spade and looked up at Wallace. 'She said it's a boy.'

Wallace said, 'Now how does she know that?'

Nora shrugged. 'She ran her hands over me. Felt around and said it. I don't know.'

In the coming weeks Wallace had trouble sleeping at night, and sometimes he would walk down into the living room of the house, where the large windows looked out over the unquiet summer dark, and on nights with a moon the sky was more blue than black and he would stand there and watch the lake. Sometimes he'd scan the trees on the roadside for the deer he knew came into the pastures at night, and sometimes he would see them, shadowy figures, a sense of movement. But mostly when he stood there, he thought about the coming baby, a boy he could hold in his arms, and he thought about how well things had gone for him, the farm was running smoothly, he had a good man in Guy, and the woman he loved was creating a child for him. It was these thoughts, finally, that brought on the elusive sleep, and he would make his way back upstairs, to his wife, to himself.

THEN, IN the second week of July, Wallace and Guy set off one morning early in the pickup truck for Saint Johnsbury and the train station. In the back of the truck they had forty-five crates of live chickens secured together by rope, though it was an awkward arrangement at best, and they drove slow so as not to knock any of the crates off. The sun had barely risen in the sky when they left, but the day was already warm and the sky was clear and cloudless. They drove in their shirtsleeves with the windows down, and the roads to Saint Johnsbury were narrow and poorly maintained and the ride was bumpy but this was a decent shipment of birds and the money would be good.

They smoked cigarettes and talked about the farm, the mild weather, talked about other farms they passed, some with herds and barns that made Wallace envious, others so ramshackle that he wondered how the inhabitants made it.

They reached the train station by midmorning and the day was now rather warm and the transaction was quick, Guy unloading the crates onto the platform while Wallace settled with the broker. He gave them sixty cents a bird, which was a fair price, and Wallace put the bills in his pocket and then helped Guy finish unloading them, the chickens nervously moving in the makeshift cages. When they were finished, they stopped quickly at the store in Saint Johnsbury and bought whiskey, beer, flour, cartons of cigarettes, sugar, and chocolate. Then they began the long drive back.

Shortly before they arrived in Eden, they saw the clouds over the mountains, and the day was so humid it seemed as if thunderstorms were inevitable. At one point Guy mentioned that they would be welcome, but Wallace had a different feeling, one he could not so easily place, but one he saw later as a premonition, as a sign, that things for him were about to change.

SHE WAS on the floor. Wallace found her, coming in the door, not seeing her outside. He found her at the precise time the sky finally gave and the rain came, falling hard on the roof, big hail-size drops. He knew, without wanting to know, what it was he was looking at. She was in the kitchen, as if she had tried to make it outside, to find someone, and her skirt was hiked up around her waist, and it was the blood he saw first, around her thighs, and then he saw it, small and bloody and undefinable, between her legs where she had passed it, and he knew without having anyone to tell him what it was. He had seen it enough with the cows to know for sure.

Wallace went to her quickly, glancing momentarily out the window to see Guy approaching the barn, oblivious to the goings-on inside the house. Nora was unconscious, but brushing his hand across her face brought her to, and he said, 'Baby, it's okay, it's okay, baby.'

She looked at him groggily. 'I'm so sorry,' she said. 'I tried.'

'I know,' Wallace said.

'It hurts so much,' said Nora, and then the tears came, down her cheeks, running fast and hard.

'I know,' he said, and he lifted her head then, brought it to his chest, and then he lifted her, wanting to take her away from this, from what they had lost.

'He wouldn't take,' Nora said.

'I know,' Wallace said, 'these things happen.'

And with that he stood her up, and then with his body between them he averted her eyes from the mess on the floor. He half-carried, half-pushed her into the living room and then upstairs. He took her into the bedroom and laid her down and she was sobbing loudly now and he said, 'I'm going to get the doctor.'

'No,' she said.

'Shush,' Wallace said and smoothed her out on the bed and kissed her.

Downstairs, Wallace took a towel from the closet, and he went to the kitchen and he picked it up, the thing from inside her, their son, her miscarriage, and he wrapped it in the soft cotton. Outside, Guy waved to him from the entrance of the barn, where he stood under the eaves smoking a cigarette, and Wallace waved back as he headed to the high pasture, the rain falling hard and erratically, soaking his shirt while the sun shone over the lake. If Guy wondered where it was he was going, he made no indication.

Wallace crossed the road and then entered the deer run, the brush running midsummer high along the sides, and he began the steady ascent up the forest wall to the fields above. He had no plan, was acting on instinct, and when he reached the pasture he hiked across it, toward the stream, and where the field doglegged to the left he followed it. He walked with the towel cradled in his arms, as one would hold a newborn. As he rounded the bend, the rain suddenly stopped, and he walked until he reached the end of the field, to the place where Nora had last year planted an apple tree, the site of their picnic, and the tree was small, barely more than a sapling, but for Wallace on this day it was a destination.

He had no tools with him, but Wallace placed the towel on the ground and with his hands began to dig. The earth was soft and wet, and he dug fast and soon he had a hole about a foot deep and a foot wide and he stopped and looked at it. It would work, he knew, and now that the practical side was accomplished, he began to cry. Wallace cried for a life that never would be lived and a son he would never have. And he cried for what would come between them now, for though he did not know what that might be, Wallace knew that something like this came between people, and he was not naïve enough to think that he and Nora were immune from it.

Into the narrow grave he placed the towel, blood now soaking through it, the stains on the outside causing him to pause for a moment, to try to discern in its shape something else, something he did not for the life of him want to know.

As the rain came again, falling at first soft and then hard, he covered the hole with the displaced dirt, pressing it into place with his hand and then with the shod toe of his leather boot. When it seemed complete to his satisfaction, Wallace looked at the dirt, at the raindrops falling on it, making soft, dimpled impressions, and he crossed himself for, though he was not religious, it seemed at the time the thing to do.

THE DOCTOR came in the afternoon. He was an old man, with a black car, a black suit, and a black bag in his hand. Wallace showed him upstairs and left him with Nora. He went outside to where Guy was feeding the pigs and told him what had happened. He saw in Guy's eyes the pain he felt himself, and once again he wanted to cry but he did not. The two men lit cigarettes and the smell of fresh manure was overpowering but Wallace did not care and they smoked in silence. Overhead the sky had cleared, and there was a soft breeze in the air.

When the doctor came out Wallace joined him in the

driveway, and the doctor looked up at Wallace and said, 'She's going to be just fine.'

'What happened?'

The doctor shrugged. 'Hard to say. Some women are just prone to it. In a few days she'll feel like herself again.'

'What does she need?'

'Rest, mostly. Feed her some steak tonight if you think of it. She lost some blood and the protein will be good for her. Other than that, most of the help she needs is with her emotions. Losing a child is a hell of a thing.'

'Thanks, Doc,' Wallace said, and the doctor shook his hand and then got in his car and headed down the dirt road toward the lake, Wallace watching until the black car rounded the bend out of sight.

That night he cooked steaks on the stove and brought Nora hers, and she said she was not hungry but he insisted and she ate anyway under his watchful eye. After she finished she rolled her head into her pillows, and he stayed with her for a moment running his hand through her hair, but she looked like she wanted to be left alone so he returned downstairs and sat out on the porch. The sky was purple with sunset, and Wallace sat out there smoking and drinking, and after a time he went back to the barn to visit with Guy, who was sitting on the edge of his cot stropping his razor blade.

Guy nodded to Wallace. 'How is she?'

'She's going to be fine.'

Guy ran the razor hard along the leather. 'How are you?'

'I've been better.'

'We going to get after more of that wood tomorrow?'

'Yeah, I think. We'll see how it is. No use doing that work if it rains.'

Back at the house Wallace shut things down and slept on the couch in the living room, not wanting to wake Nora and figuring she needed her sleep. In the morning when he rose, she was still asleep and he went to her, sat on the edge of the bed, and she opened her eyes and looked at him, and she began to cry and he pushed her hair away from where it fell across her forehead. Wallace moved to hug her, but she rolled away from him and into the pillow, and after a minute he heard her sobs stop. With his hand he squeezed her thigh beneath the sheets, and then he ran one hand through her hair.

'It's going to be okay, baby,' Wallace said.

But she did not respond. Wallace squeezed her thigh again, and then he stood and went downstairs to make coffee on the stove, to do the milking.

For a week Nora barely left bed. Wallace brought her food and tried to bring her out of her shell, but her sorrow was deep and he did not know how to reach her. After that first morning he stopped giving her hugs even, for her aloofness had grown more complete, and Wallace knew he should do something to pull her out, to help make her whole but, by and large, he left her alone.

Wallace simply delved into the work there was to be done, surprising Guy with his intensity, rising earlier in the morning, working later into the night. During that week they built an entire new shed behind the barn, a simple structure made of old wood that they slapped red paint on, and in which they stored equipment that had been displaced when they expanded the chicken operation in the large barn. While they worked, they did not talk, it was as if they reverted to where they were months before, when Guy first arrived. They were strangers again, oddly, and Wallace knew it was his fault, that Guy was simply giving him his space, as he was giving space to Nora, though he also knew that it could have longer implications, this strangeness, this moving inward to his thoughts.

One warm morning Guy and Wallace were putting a finishing coat on the shed when Wallace looked up and saw Nora. She wore a long white dress and her hair was down and he thought she might be barefoot, though it was hard to tell at this distance. He watched as she moved from the back door of the house out to the kitchen garden and then into it, sinking to her knees, and he could see her weeding and it made him happy. He was tempted to go to her then, but he did not, he went back to his painting, lifting his eyes every few minutes to see her working in the garden. After a time, they quit for lunch, and on his way back to the house Wallace stopped and Nora looked up at him where she kneeled, and in front of her on the ground were some small carrots, some new potatoes.

'Hi,' said Wallace.

'Hi.'

'Good-looking potatoes.'

'Yes.'

Wallace wiped his brow with his sleeve. 'Quite a day. God's weather.'

Nora looked up at the sky, clear and blue. 'Yes.'

'Can I get you some lunch?'

'No,' said Nora. 'I think I will just stay out here for a while.'

And so Wallace left her there, in the garden, the garden with its fertile soil that prodigiously produced all manner of vegetables. He left her there and went inside and ate lunch. And while he ate, he thought about how happy he was that she seemed to be coming back. Her gardening was a good sign that she was kicking out of the grief. What he did not know then was that it was only the beginning. He knew that the miscarriage was something that had suddenly come between them, but he figured like all things it would heal in time. And, in truth, it did, at least that part of it. But he knew that all he had buried in the ground at the base of the apple tree was a fetus. The rest of it was still in the world, and Wallace had no idea how to push it away, to bring back her love.

10

Wallace told me the story of Nora's miscarriage on a bleak day in early December, sitting in front of the woodstove, and seeing his ancient eyes grow wet I fought back tears as outside the snow flurries fell to the hard ground. A few days later, something curious happened.

I was at the post office and had not yet gone out on my route. I was sorting the mail into the bins I used for each section of Eden, when I noticed a thin letter addressed to Nora Fiske. It had no return address, and her name was written in ink, with an unsteady hand, and while it was not entirely unusual for the deceased to receive mail, generally it happened the first six months to a year after the death, not five years. By that point, pretty much all the direct mail companies and everyone else has figured out that that person is no longer alive.

For a minute I actually thought about opening the letter, which was a clear violation of postal regulations, a federal crime, in fact, but I had a burning itch to know who would be writing to Nora Fiske. As soon as I dismissed that idea, I thought of simply bringing the letter to Wallace, but ingrained in my mind was the image of Wallace and our first meeting, his hatred of the mail, and I also remembered how he burned what little I brought him in the stove without so much as opening it.

So instead what I did was get on the phone and call the main branch in Montpelier, and tell them about getting a deceased person's mail long after she had died. What they told me in return is what shocked me.

After an interminable period of time when the woman on the other end of the line went to check the records, she finally came back and said, 'Nathan?'

'Yes?'

'Yeah. That one should have been rerouted. If you want to send it back with the afternoon truck, I'll take care of it.'

'Rerouted? What do you mean?'

'There's a forwarding address. Every six months it's been renewed. Bit of a pain in the ass, really. Somehow that letter didn't get caught. It happens.'

This had to be a mistake. I said, 'Can I have that address? Just in case another one comes here or something.'

When we had hung up, I looked at the note in my hand. The forwarding address was to Bliss Road, Jay, New York. Connie had an atlas on her desk, and I opened it to the map of New York State, used the little numbers and letters to find out the location of Jay, which as it turns out is across Lake Champlain in the high peaks region of the Adirondacks.

That night Kate cooked me dinner at my place and we ate pasta with mushrooms and cream and while we did I told her what I had found out.

'Do you really think it's the same person?'

I said, 'Must be. I mean, why else would it come to Wallace's?'

'Why do you think he told you she died?'

'I don't know. Perhaps he is embarrassed that she left him. Hard to say.'

'You should go there . . .'

'Go there?'

'To New York, meet Nora.'

'That's a little extreme, don't you think?'

'Telling you your wife is dead when she's alive is a little extreme, Nathan.'

The following morning was a Saturday, and I did my route earlier than usual and then went and picked up Kate at Linger's. The sky was overcast, and some light snow flurries fell to the ground. Kate and I drove northeast to Route 89, and in Grand Isle we turned off and drove on a narrow winding highway that took us past inlets on the lake where men ice-fished in shacks. Soon we reached the ferry landing to cross Lake Champlain, and the iron gray lake lay in front of us, about three miles across at this point, and on the opposite shore I could make out a town, the steeple of a church, some industrial buildings, houses close to the water.

The ferry was a small boat, a barge really, with a flat deck for cars and a small upper deck that included the captain's cabin. We had to wait for only a few minutes before the steward signaled us onto the ferry, and we drove on, parked the Jeep, and got out. We climbed to the upper deck with the dozen or so other passengers and, though there was a small room in which to stand sheltered from the cold, Kate and I stood outside and smoked cigarettes and watched as the ferry noise-lessly left the dock and began to move out into the lake. Soon we had left shore behind and the wind picked up and blew strongly across the deck and in the water below we could see that we were cutting through floating chunks of gray ice. Looking south the lake widened near Burlington, and we could see tiny islands dotting the surface, at this time of year nothing more than floating snow against the darkness of the water. We could also see the white-capped high peaks of the Adirondacks, our destination, where it now appeared Nora Fiske lived.

After about fifteen minutes we could no longer stand the cold and we were close to the opposite shore anyway so we returned to the Jeep and climbed in and I turned on the heat. In front of us we watched as the steward threw a rope to another man in the same Eskimo jacket and red hat on the shore and they roped the ferry off and it swayed for a minute before settling in and then they opened the gates and we drove off.

We drove into a small town and through the center of it and, though the landscape was very similar here to the other side, you could already see that you were no longer in Vermont, the quaint feel giving way to a gritty, more hardscrabble quality.

Outside of Plattsburgh we stopped and ate burgers at a diner and then just as quickly were back in the car again, driving south on a narrow highway, Kate doing the navigating. Going south, the flat farmland grew more wooded, and we passed though dense woods and higher country, the monotony of the road split up by small towns, less gritty now and more touristy, signs here and there for antiques shops and for Adirondack furniture, most of them shuttered closed for the winter. Near Keene, the sun finally broke though the gray sky, and it was suddenly beautiful, the sunlight playing off the snow and the forest of evergreens, and at one point we rounded a bend and it almost took my breath away, the sheer beauty of the sight in front of us, Whiteface Mountain rising out of the trees above a gulch formed by the Ausable River that now ran alongside the road, its boulder-strewn bottom covered with thick, white ice.

Jay, New York, as it turned out, you could have missed if you blinked. It was little more than a collection of houses, a church, and a general store, and by the time we arrived there the sun was heading down, the December day quickly passing, and since there appeared to be no place to stay, we turned back the way we came to Keene, where we had passed a bed-and-breakfast with a vacancy sign.

A large man in his early sixties took our money and led us to our room on the second floor, which was in the front of the house and looked out onto the rural highway we had driven down. He suggested the best place for dinner was Lake Placid, which was about ten miles north, and so after taking showers we got back in the car and drove through the dark on a winding road that took us through Wilmington, and then past Whiteface Mountain, lights from the ski hill barely visible in the dark. Then we drove through a dense forest, around hairpin turns on a road that suddenly narrowed in places and was lined with stone walls. I remarked to Kate, 'On the way back, this is going to be a sobriety test.'

We found an Italian restaurant on the main street and were given a table in front of a window overlooking the frozen lake, the part in front of the houses on the opposite shore lit up and shoveled free of snow, ice-skaters moving in circles on it, giving me for an instant the illusion that we were in another country, Holland, say.

We each had linguine with clams and ordered a bottle of Chianti, and the pasta was warm and good and the clams sweet. Sitting across from Kate and getting high on the red wine, I had that sudden urge to make love to her, and she must have seen it in my face because she smiled at me, twirling the pasta with her fork and her spoon, her foot coming up under the table and rubbing against my leg.

Back at the bed-and-breakfast – the trip, as I imagined, a little hairy, headlights around the corner causing me to hit my brakes, relieved when the car passed and the road was ours again – we opened more wine upstairs and then we crept down the dark stairs and into the kitchen.

'Should we be here?' I said.

'Shush,' said Kate, and in the freezer we found ice cream and I brought it over to the table and found us each spoons and, before we could eat, Kate inexplicably took off her shirt, and I chuckled, for she sat bare-breasted before me, oblivious to the fact that the owner could have come out at any moment or, more likely, aware of it and not caring, and for that I loved her. We sat and ate ice cream out of the tub, both of us with our own spoons, Kate with her shirt off, her breasts slightly giving way to the realities of gravity, but beautiful nonetheless, with that slight slope upward and her nipples in front of me in the half-dark, and it was bold and sexy, and with each scoop of ice cream into her mouth she dramatically ran her tongue along the spoon, teasing me, and I remember thinking that this is a woman who knows how to live, for whom the moment is everything, so different from myself, caught up in the future and the past at the same time, the present as elusive as true love itself.

In time we made our way upstairs, and in the dark she undressed me and I felt her warm mouth around me and when she came up I lay her alongside me and slid into her from behind, and outside we heard an occasional car on the highway beyond the window, and we made love slowly this way. After, when Kate drifted off with her head on my chest, I lay there until sleep, too, overtook me, and while I did I thought of tomorrow, of Nora, of Wallace, of a house overlooking Mirror Lake, and I wondered if I would discover what it was I yearned to know: where their love went bad, and what it was that caused it.

THE NEXT day a wan winter sun barely fought through the grayness and it was terribly cold when Kate and I set out to find Nora Fiske. We drove back the way we had gone the day before, down to Jay, and past the church we stopped at a general store and asked the way to Bliss Road, and the fat man behind the counter told us it was the second right past the pond and sure enough there it was, marked by a green sign. The road curved up and away from the highway, and there were no houses, only deep woods, and the road was snow-covered and slick and we drove slowly. The road graded steadily higher, and soon the woods gave way to an open plateau along our left that stretched to the high peaks, Mount Marcy in the middle, and even in the thin December light it was a spectacular view.

We had been driving for about five minutes when I realized that we had yet to see a house. On our left was just the endless open plateau, and on our right was woods, but soon that, too, opened to fields, and the wind blew hard and fast across them and blew the snow from the ground into the air, where it lingered for a moment in tiny cyclones.

Around a sharp bend the woods began again, and set back from the road was a two-story farmhouse, gray and weathered with a wraparound porch, an evergreen forest behind it, the trees all of uniform size, planted close together, and behind them were small rolling foothills, and in a break between two of them we could see a flat-topped mountain, its summit partially obscured by white clouds.

'I bet this is it,' said Kate.

We stopped the Jeep in front of the driveway, which was long and led to the back of the house. There were no lights visible inside the house, and no sign of a car. The driveway was snow-covered and had no tracks. On the opposite side of the road, though, there was a mailbox, and I got out of the Jeep and went to it. Sure enough, written in block letters on the side was the one word I was looking for. FISKE.

Back in the Jeep I turned and said to Kate, 'Bingo.'

We pulled partway into the driveway and got out. There was still no sign of anyone in the farmhouse or around it.

I said, 'What do you think?'

'Check the door, I guess.'

Slowly the two of us walked to the house, and when we reached the porch we could see that it was in worse shape than it appeared at a distance, shingles falling off, others badly in need of a fresh coat of battleship gray paint. The front door itself had once been red but was now rust-colored and paint-chipped with a large crack cut diagonally across the top panel, the middle of which went clear through. I reached my hand up and rapped several times on the door. No response. I looked at Kate. Then I tried again, banging harder now, and we both stepped back and waited.

'Doesn't sound like anyone's home,' Kate said.

'Should we wait?'

'We came all the way here.'

We leaned against the rail of the porch, and I fumbled in my pockets for my cigarettes and my lighter and lit Kate and myself each one and we stood there smoking, looking out over the open land at the woods and the mountains. The wind blew hard here, but it was not as cold as you might think, strong enough to blow our hair back but not quite cold enough to drive us back into the sanctuary of the Jeep. From time to time the weak sun emerged in the gray sky, and the light it cast was diffused and indirect, as if covered by a large piece of opaque paper.

As soon as we had finished our cigarettes I thought I heard something from behind the house and I stepped off the porch and for the first time I saw Nora Fiske, not as I had imagined her, not the woman in the pictures, but an old woman, bundled up against the cold, a hat on her head, a scarf wrapped around her neck and the lower part of her face, covering her mouth. She was probably thirty yards behind the house, moving toward us, though she had not yet seen us, or the Jeep. She wore snowshoes on her feet, and at this distance she looked remarkably small, and frail, a perception tempered in part by the fact that her arms were overflowing with cordwood. She looked like she might tip over.

I stepped out farther and called 'hello,' and she looked up and saw me, but might as well not have, for she said nothing in return, and kept her steady pace across the snow, disappearing from view behind the house.

I joined Kate again on the porch, and I shrugged my shoulders, as if to say, What now? But before we could do anything, the front door opened, and she stood in front of us, a diminutive woman, her hair a shiny gray and hanging halfway down her back. Her eyes were small and dark and her face was wrinkled, but up close now I knew without a doubt it was her; I knew that if I could somehow have washed away the years, I would have been looking at the same woman that lay on a blanket drinking beer at a midday summer picnic, Wallace behind her, a woman who once had brown hair and wet eyes and a wide smile.

I said, 'Nora Fiske?' Her eyes moved from me to Kate, then back to me again.

'Yes,' she said.

'My name is Nathan Carter, and this is Kate.'

'What is it you want?'

'We are friends of Wallace's.'

'Wallace doesn't have any friends.'

'Well, I should say that I am a friend of Wallace's.'

'Is he dead?'

'Oh, no. He's fine.'

'Then why are you here?'

'That,' I said, 'I don't know.'

INSIDE WE sat in rocking chairs in front of the woodstove while Nora made tea somewhere in the back. The room was low-ceilinged and small, and sparsely decorated, a few chairs, an old couch, a chest as a coffee table. There was no television, though stacked against one wall was a pile of old hard-covered books. The few windows were covered with heavy drapes, and though it was early afternoon, it was very dark in there, the only light coming from the fire visible through the glass of the woodstove, shadows flickering off the walls behind us. Kate and I sat in silence, looking at the fire, looking around the room, and in a few minutes Nora came back in with a tray in her hands, which she put down on the chest. She then poured us each a cup of tea and handed them to us.

I started by explaining how I knew Wallace, our battle over the mail, my car accident, our developing and growing friendship.

I told her how he eventually opened up and told me about her, their life together, their marriage. I did not tell her that he'd told me she was dead. I told her that he'd had a heart attack, though he was okay now, back working at the farm. Throughout my telling, Nora sat across from me with her hands folded in her lap, expressionless. None of this seemed to faze her, or be especially of interest. When I had finished, she paused for a minute, looked at me and then at the fire. I followed her eyes.

'And he told you I was here?' she asked.

'No. He told me you had passed away.'

She nodded. 'That makes sense.'

I told her how I had found her, and apologized for just showing up, but said that I needed to know if it was indeed her and, more important, why it was that Wallace, who spoke so eloquently and deeply about their life together, would tell me that she was dead, when in fact she was not, as her presence in front of me clearly indicated.

Nora looked down at her hands for a long while before answering me. 'There's no reason I should tell you this,' she said.

'You don't have to,' I said.

She continued to look down at her hands, and then, as if trying to compose herself, she sat up straight in the chair, patted the back of her hair down. 'Wallace and I became dead to each other long ago,' she said. 'That's why.'

'But Wallace said you were the love of his life.'

'I was.'

I thought about pressing this point, but decided not to. I

sat back and looked at her, at this little woman living alone in the woods here, her shiny gray hair falling down over the back of the chair. I realized that we should not have come, that this was a fool's trip, better to let sleeping dogs lie, as it were. I was about to apologize and thank her for the tea and make a graceful exit when she said, 'But he was not mine.'

'Not your what?'

'The love of my life.'

'No?'

'No,' she said, looking first at Kate, back to me, down to her lap, her voice growing softer as she said, 'Guy was.'

The rest of that afternoon is largely a blur now, obscured by the revelation that Nora loved Guy, and that Guy loved Nora. We stayed late into the evening, and she talked hour after hour, telling us what she could, what I realize now she was ready for us to know. Kate and I drove back to Eden in silence, and it was a white-knuckle ride, since by the time we left Jay the snow was falling hard and it was dark, almost whiteout conditions on the highway, but curiously enough I was grateful for the difficult driving conditions, something to focus on, something besides a betrayal of love, besides a cuckolded Wallace.

11

Like many things, it started innocently enough. It was not love at first sight. Rather it grew slowly, building over time, eventually taking on a life of its own, an inevitability from which there was no return. I wanted to ask her if she were to do it over would she do it the same way, but I knew that question was fundamentally unfair, for though she may not have regretted the love she had, who among us would not do things differently if given the chance? Who among us would not at least change something in our past? But I know now that it does not work that way, for to change something is to change everything, nothing exists in complete isolation, each action is connected to the next: remove one and the whole thing unravels. Wallace taught me that. And I'm not sure I'm glad I know it. I live a lot more deliberately as a result.

Its roots could be traced, most likely, to Guy's arrival on the farm. Though she says it was not love at first sight, I can only imagine that there was something between them that day when she took him into the farmhouse, showed him the room she had created above the barn, brought him up to meet Wallace. Perhaps it was not much, a slightly palpable tension, barely on the surface, but there nonetheless. Or perhaps it is as she says it was, that at that time she did not even conceive of betraying Wallace, that he was her world, and she his, and she saw Guy as nothing more than a man in ragged clothes, someone who needed work, a place to sleep; just as they needed someone to fill a void left by Wallace's illness; a void defined by work, not by love or need; that would come later and be particular to her.

THERE WERE, Nora said, his eyes to consider, which were dark and serpentine, narrow, yet the most intense she had ever seen. Those late winter nights when Wallace lay up in bed and the two of them sat together at the kitchen table, talking and joking, Guy drinking whiskey, she was struck by his eyes, alternately beautiful and sinister, she did not know which. Sometimes she would look up quickly and see his eyes moving away from her, and she sensed that they had been on her breasts, her throat, and she knew enough about men to know that this was not unusual; but his gaze in that half second before he looked away was forceful, and she found herself thinking about it at night when she lay next to Wallace. Sometimes, as well, she thought she imagined it, his gaze, as if she wanted him to look at her that way, as if she wanted someone to look at her that way.

One night at the table Guy told her about Michelle and Potvin and his time in Montreal. And she wept when he finished, and as she looked across at him she thought he was the most beautiful man she had ever seen, his eyes, the strength of his jawline, his comfort with himself and with her.

'That's the saddest story I've ever heard,' Nora said.

'Love is often sad,' said Guy.

Nora looked at his hands, cupped in front of her on the wooden table, and they were strong and delicate at the same time. 'Would you love her again? Knowing how things turned out?'

Guy smiled. 'Of course. There are things that are bigger than all of us. Love is one. The land is another. At the time, I felt like, I don't know, I felt like I needed to fight for her. Fighting for a woman is something to fight for, no?'

'Yes,' said Nora. 'I think that is right. But you lost. It's so sad.'

'But maybe I won something else.'

'I don't know. You're here. And not with her.'

'But maybe this is a victory. We will never know. I was raised to believe that things happen for a reason. Maybe I'm here for a reason, then.'

Nora thought about this, and she thought that maybe he was right. That maybe he was here for her, because of her. But then just as quickly she dismissed it, because she knew she had to, and as she looked away to escape the intensity of his eyes, she tried to imagine having this conversation with

Wallace, and she decided that she could not, that Guy was different, Guy with his clipped Québecois accent, his intense, dark eyes, his confidence. She knew then that she would have to be careful with him, that she liked her time with him more than she wanted to admit, looked forward to it, in fact, and as she thought this she felt guilt, for Wallace was upstairs in bed and she owed him more than the comfort of another man.

AND,THEN, that spring, she got pregnant, and any thoughts of anything other than the life growing within her faded away. It was a brief time, those several months, but Nora would remember it as perhaps the time she was happiest. Wallace was healthy again, the farm was prosperous, there was Guy for company, and then there was the prospect of the baby, something she did not realize she wanted so badly until it happened to her, and then the idea of it consumed her in a way she could not have envisioned. She liked to press her fingers into the soft flesh of her belly and feel the push back of a little foot, or a hand, she could not know which. She liked the way she looked in the mirror, when she stood in front of it in the morning after Wallace had left, her silhouette growing perceptibly larger each passing day, running her hands over her stomach, the way her breasts seemed to rest on it. She liked the blush in her cheeks, and for the first time in her life she felt beautiful, really beautiful, as if the child within had suddenly created the woman without, and not vice versa. And mostly Nora liked the feeling of significance she had, as if she was taking up more space, which of course she was, but something deeper than that, a feeling of purpose, of motherhood.

Sometimes she had pain, like the morning sickness, which came not just in the morning but at night, too, driving her from bed to the washroom, where she leaned over the basin retching until it happened. But that was early and soon passed, and the midwife came and looked at her and she had no reason to believe that anything could go wrong. The morning that Wallace and Guy brought the chickens to Saint Johnsbury was like any other summer morning, except that it was warm, very warm, and doing the chores around the house she felt at times slightly dizzy and faint, and at one point she sat down in the chair in the living room and she felt like she might be sick, and then the cramps started, deep and low in her belly, and she tried to stand but she could not. She doubled over in pain and somehow managed to sit back down. She tried to think. Perhaps it was only cramps, like she used to have with her menstruation. But the pain continued to grow in intensity, and she had a sudden urge to be outside, a panicky feeling, and this time was able to stand, making it as far as the kitchen before the pain took her down again, this time to the floor, where she lay, suddenly grateful for the cool wood beneath her legs.

The pain was so strong Nora wanted to cry out but could not. She lay there, and while she did it occurred to her for the first time what was happening. She realized she was about to lose the baby, and as soon as she thought it her stomach muscles began to contract, almost against her will, and she could feel it, inside her, moving down, and with her hand she felt the first blood between her legs, and in that moment the pain shot through her like white heat, and her legs opened, and she felt it now, in her hands, soft and hard at the same time, sticky, and the pain and sorrow converged at once, too much for her to handle alone. She passed out.

In the days that followed Nora fell into something that decades later she was still unable to describe. It was grief, sure, but it was more than that, too; a sense of loss that went beyond the loss of the child. She knew she needed to bring herself out of it, but she did not know how. Wallace was there for her, doing everything he could, but somewhere inside herself she was angry with him. Nora knew it was irrational, but she could not help it. She felt that he had abandoned her that morning, that morning when she needed him more than she had ever needed anyone. Most of all she felt empty, for just as her womb was now empty, for reasons she could not fully comprehend her love had gone empty, too, so that she and Wallace were now going through the motions, the daily work and rituals that collectively constitute a shared life, and for the first time since she had met him, Nora had a yearning and a need that could not be filled within the context of the two of them. She did not at that time intend for Guy to fill it. It just happened this way.

A WARM afternoon in August, Nora was in the garden, weeding between the tomato plants, when suddenly he was there. He and Wallace had been far up on the land, in the high pasture with the horses, tilling new land to plant winter rye. Nora had not expected to see either of them until late, for the work was arduous and Wallace liked to do it all at once.

'Hello,' said Guy.

Nora looked up. 'Hi,' she said, and she found that she was smiling, surprising herself with how glad she was to see him. 'I didn't expect to see the two of you until late.'

'Wallace is still up there. I came to get some grease. The hinge on the plow keeps catching.'

Nora nodded and looked down at her hands, a thin layer of dirt covering them. Guy sat down in the grass next to the garden, took out his rolling papers and his tobacco, and rolled a cigarette. 'You can tell it's coming,' he said.

'It?'

'Fall.'

'Yes. It comes so quickly here.'

Guy lighted his cigarette, inhaled, leaned back. 'You are good at that. The garden. Look at those tomatoes. They shouldn't be so big, no? I don't think I've ever seen tomatoes like that. Perfect.'

Nora laughed. 'All that Jersey manure. That's the secret.'

'Beautiful things grow from shit.'

'I hope so,' Nora said.

'Are you okay?'

Nora looked over at him. 'What do you mean?'

'I don't know. The summer. It's been hard on you, I can tell.'

Nora looked across the fields to the road, the woods on the other side, up to where she knew Wallace was working. She wanted to say something, but did not.

Guy continued, 'I'm sorry, I should mind my business.'

Nora said, 'No, you're right. It has been hard. But things are better now.'

'Good. That's the way it should be. I'm sorry to bother you. I should get back to work.'

Guy rose to his feet, dropping his cigarette, mashing it into the grass with his boot.

'Thanks,' Nora said.

'For what?'

'For checking on me, if that's what you were doing.'

'I have had hard times,' he said. 'I know what it is like. Any time you want to talk.'

Nora nodded and watched as he headed off, toward the barn, and she watched him walk, his sure gait, steady and strong, and for a second she wondered what it would be like to feel his hands on her, and then she stopped herself, and when he came back out of the barn on his way to the pasture, an oilcan in his hand, she pretended not to see him and busied herself by working her hands through the warm, dry soil beneath her.

ON A NIGHT when the moon was almost full and the land was white with its light, Nora went to him. Wallace had drunk heavily after dinner, and his snoring kept her awake until she needed to do something. She crept down the stairs and into the living room, and then from the kitchen she could see out the windows to the moonlit pastureland, and beyond it the barn, and in the small window on the second floor she could see

Guy's light. She stood watching the fields, the dark, shadowy shapes of the Jerseys still out there, standing in huddled packs, and eventually she slid her rubber mud boots on, aware of how she must have looked in her nightgown with boots, her flesh visible from above her knee to midway down her calf.

Nora opened the door and stood listening. She heard the night sounds, crickets, mostly, but nothing from upstairs. Slowly she stepped outside and began to walk across the lawn and then across the pasture. The moon sat above the lake behind her, and its light was almost like daylight, so that she could see perfectly as she made her way past the cows, the woodpile, and the sugar shack. At the barn she paused and listened again, and it was silent in there, and slowly she opened the large doors enough so that she could slip through, and inside it was dark though through the rafters she could see the lights from Guy's room. She made her way across the earthen floor to the ladder that led to it, and she was on the second rung when she looked up and saw his face in the square hole, his dark eyes and hair framed by the light behind him.

'I'm sorry,' Nora said, almost a whisper. 'I hope this is okay.'

'Of course, of course. Come up.'

She climbed two more rungs and then took Guy's outstretched hand, felt its chapped palm against her own, and let him half-pull her up the rest of the way.

It was the first time Nora had been in the room since she created it, back in the cold of January, when Wallace was ill and she needed something to keep her busy. It looked largely the same, though lived in, an oil lamp lit on the table next to the bed, work clothes slung over the back of a chair. The lamp shot fingers of light up the old wood walls, and the window that looked out over the pasture had cobwebs in the corners of it. Nora was unsure what to do with herself once she was up here, but then Guy cleared a place on the bed for her and she sat down and he sat next to her, about two feet away. She looked at her feet, her boots.

'I shouldn't have come,' she said.

'I'm glad you did.'

'I couldn't sleep.'

'You don't have to explain.'

'Wallace would think this is crazy.'

'It's not.'

'I hope so. I can't tell.'

'You wanted someone to talk to, no?'

'Yes.'

'Well, that is it. We're talking. That is okay.'

'I suppose so.'

'Do you want some cider?'

'Are you having any?'

'Yes.'

'Yes, then.'

Guy stood and went over to the woodstove, and Nora watched as he leaned down behind it and pulled up a heavy clay jug. He put it on top of the stove and then reached down and came up with two small glasses. He poured the cider into each one and then handed one to her. It was hard and she could smell the fermented alcohol before it hit her lips, and she sipped it slowly and it was strong but it was what she needed.

Guy sat back next to her, closer this time, and she found that she could not look at him. Instead she looked at the floor-boards, at her maroon cider in the cup in her hands. They sat in silence for a moment until the silence seemed more oppres-sive than words, and it was Nora who spoke first.

She said, 'What are you doing here?'

'What do you mean?'

'Here. This lake. This farm. With Wallace and me.'

'I don't know. I needed work. You needed help. Does it have to be any more complicated than that?'

'Sometimes I feel alone, even though I'm not. I feel like there has to be something more than this. At one time this is all I wanted. To get married, be here, be a farmer's wife. Lately I've wanted to go somewhere, nowhere in particular, either. It's strange.'

'So why don't you?'

'Go somewhere?'

'Yes.'

'You can't just do that. I mean, you could. You have nothing that holds you here. With me, it's different. I have Wallace and the house and with that come obligations. It's probably just me. When I was teaching I wanted out of that, too. Maybe I'm one of those people who doesn't know how to be happy.'

'I'm not sure if anyone is ever truly happy. You have to find the little things that give you pleasure. Tobacco. Hard work. A swim in summer. Your garden. That seems to make you happy, no?'

Nora shook her head. 'I guess. I like seeing it come together, seeing the vegetables grow, and it's my own thing, separate from the work that Wallace does, though we both eat what comes out of there. I don't know. I'm sorry, Guy, it's late and I'm bothering you with crazy talk.'

'It's not crazy. You'll see. We all think these things. We all wonder what would happen if we made different choices. You have a good life, Nora. And you're a strong woman. A beautiful woman. Good things happen to beautiful women, I think.'

Nora looked up at him then and smiled, and Guy smiled, too, his face dimpling as he looked back at her. She wanted to touch him, he was so close to her, but there was a distance between them, and then he did, touched her, his course hand on the bare skin on the back of her neck, and she closed her eyes, and she felt his other hand on her shoulder, and then his breath on the side of her throat, the hard muscle of his thigh against hers.

'No,' she said.

Guy sat back, his hand leaving her neck, her shoulder, though she still felt their presence there. Nora opened her eyes and looked over at him. She said, 'I can't.'

'I know.'

'I wish –'

'Don't.'

Nora sipped her cider. 'I should go. I don't want Wallace to wake and wonder where I am. I don't think he would understand this.'

'It's our secret.'

'I shouldn't have come. I was lonely, but that is no excuse.'

'We just talked.'

'Yes.'

'People can talk, no?'

'Yes, people can talk.'

Outside a front had moved in and clouds now obscured the moon, and Nora walked gingerly through the fields, past the sleeping cows, toward the quiet house. Before going in she walked briefly around front and stood looking down at Mirror Lake, black in the deep night, and off in the distance she could make out a light on Foster Hill, and she realized it was most likely the light from the house where she used to live before Wallace, when she taught school and things were simpler.

Inside the house she crept back up the stairs, and slowly opened the door to the room she shared with Wallace, and he was on his side, his snores audible even out in the hallway, and as she lowered herself onto the mattress, his snores stopped for a quick second, but then they began again, and she lay there on her back, looking up at the ceiling, and while she did she thought of Guy out in the barn, and she remembered the feel of his hands, the feel of his want, inexpressible but there nonetheless, and she thought of this until she fell asleep, and the thinking of it made her happy.

THERE WAS awkwardness between them after that, though they did not acknowledge it and went on as if Nora had never visited him in the dead of night, as if his hands were never on her. In late summer Wallace and Guy hayed the fields, and the days were longer than usual and one night Wallace brought Guy back for dinner and they were in a good mood because it was a good day, good weather and they got most of the top field done, and Nora cooked for them, roast chicken and corn, tomato salad. After, the men drank whiskey and Nora took some too, and while they sat on the porch watching the sun leave the sky and watching the lake, flat and still, Nora stole glances at Guy, the firmness of his jaw, those narrow, intense eyes, and sometimes she caught him looking at her and it pleased her. But then when it grew dark, Wallace signaled he was ready for bed, and Guy stood and said his goodbyes and Nora watched as he rounded the corner of the house, and she bit her lip for she wanted to go with him but knew she could not.

Then it was September and the nights grew cool and the first leaves in the trees started to change. One afternoon Wallace came to her and said he was going to ride into Montpelier and look at a new truck. He asked her if she wanted to go.

'We could maybe get some dinner there,' he said. Then when she declined he seemed puzzled. 'You always wanted to go to Montpelier if I was going. Well, I'm going.'

'I know,' Nora said, 'I just don't feel right today.'

'Suit yourself.'

Wallace had been gone for only ten minutes when she saw Guy out the window, returning from the high pasture, and she signaled to him out the window and he saw and came to the door.

'Wallace is going to Montpelier,' she said.

'I know.'

'I hate to eat alone.'

Guy smiled. 'Sounds like you want company.'

'Yes, can you come?'

'Let me clean up,' he said.

In an hour he returned, and Nora opened the door for him, his hair slicked back and wet, and in his left hand he held a single flower, a red rose.

'That looks familiar,' she said.

'It's yours.'

'In more ways than one.'

Inside, they ate a dinner of corn, pepper, and onions slow-cooked in butter, pork chops cooked in cider, and some dandelion greens tossed with apple cider vinegar. After, they drank whiskey on the porch and Guy smoked. They talked little during dinner and less after, as if each was aware of the stakes of the game they played, and neither quite understood how to take it to the next step. Eventually, with the sun setting and the evening warm, Nora took charge as she knew she had to, and turned to Guy and said, 'I need to swim.'

Together they walked down to Mirror Lake, towels over their shoulders, and in her mind Nora calculated when Wallace would be back. She figured at the earliest two hours, though more likely three. At the bottom of the hill they cut through a path lined with tall grasses to the lakeshore. They put their towels down on a large rock, and the lake was right in front of them, still and flat as glass, dragonflies zooming across its surface. Nora took off her dress, pulling it over her head, and underneath she wore a bra and a slip, and out of the corner of her eye she saw Guy remove his shirt and then his pants, standing there in his boxer shorts, and without a word she waded quickly into the water, and when it was waist high she dived forward, her arms outstretched, hitting the water and sliding under it, closing her eyes, pushing her arms away from in front of her, propelling herself forward out into the lake. She surfaced about thirty feet offshore, wiped her hair away from her forehead, and then Guy popped up next to her, laughing.

'Shit, that's nice,' he said.

They trod water about a foot away from each other, and she looked at him until she could not anymore, then she swam away from him, farther out into the lake, and behind her she could hear him coming, and then felt him, his hands around her waist for a second, before she squirmed away and swam even farther out. This time she did not hear him, and she turned around and she saw that he had not moved from their last spot.

'I give up,' he shouted to her. 'You are too hard to catch.'

'You barely tried,' Nora said.

Guy raised his hands in the air in mock exasperation. 'What am I to do? You are too fast, too slippery.'

Nora shook her head at him and swam still farther out, till she was halfway across, and when she spun this time he was almost to shore, walking now in water partway up his belly. She stayed out there for a minute, looking across the surface of the lake to the tooth-shaped peninsula on the far side, to the evergreens along the eastern shore, rising quickly up with the hillside, dense, green trees. She looked back at Guy, who was standing now on the lakeshore, toweling himself off. And then she began to swim in a crawl, her arms in front of her, cutting through the water, feeling the strength of the muscles in her shoulders as they motored her, pleased with the sobering physicality of swimming fast.

At the shore she climbed out, Guy sitting on a rock in front of her, watching her, and she was aware of how she must have looked to him, and she could see it in his eyes as he took her in, her wet hair, her wet underwear clinging to her body, her nipples visible beneath the cotton of her bra. He threw her the other towel, and she caught it, dried herself off, and then slung her dress over her arm, not bothering to put it back on, and together they walked up the small hill to the house.

On the porch she sat on the bench while Guy poured them each more whiskey. The swim had taken an hour, and she figured the earliest they would see Wallace was an hour from now. When Guy returned he sat next to her, and Nora suddenly shuddered with cold from the swim and the alcohol, and then she felt his hand on her neck, and she turned to him, turned quickly to him, with goose bumps on her arms, and he kissed her, kissed her lips, and she returned his kiss, and she felt his hand now on the nape of her neck, and she welcomed it, his kissing, and she thought: I can't sleep with him. But the more they kissed, sitting on the porch in the dark, she felt her will go out of her, and when he stood and pulled her up after him, led her by the hand out onto the soft, dewy grass in front of the house, laid a towel on the ground and pulled her down onto it, on top of him, she had no thoughts but the moment.

And so it was that on a late summer night, on the front lawn of the house she shared with her husband, another man moved inside her. Nora kept her eyes shut the entire time, moving on top of him as if by instinct, his hands supporting her on her shoulders. It was beautiful and low, and in her mind she saw the waves of the lake slapping against the shore and in her mind she felt his fullness inside her and in her mind she saw herself on him, swallowing him with warmth.

When he had finished, she rolled off of him and onto her back next to him, the grass wet and cold against her skin. She looked up at the stars and she felt Guy's hand now on her belly, and she could not look at him, not in that moment, but then she did, his eyes on her, a look she recognized from her early time with Wallace, a look of love, and she told herself to hold it in, but she could not, and lying there with the stars above she began to cry.

'It's okay,' Guy said, running his hands through her hair, moving it out of her face.

'It's not you,' Nora said. 'Sometimes making love makes me weep.'

'I know,' he said, and rose up onto his elbows, so that he was looking down on her and she up at him.

'We should go,' she said.

'No.'

'Wallace will be home.'

'I don't care. I don't care about anything like that.'

'You have to, for me, you have to.'

'I know,' Guy said. 'But that doesn't mean I have to like it.'

She watched Guy walk all the way into the barn from the corner of the house, and she stayed there until she saw the light of his oil lamp in the upstairs window. Inside she washed the dishes from dinner, put them into the drying rack, knowing that Wallace would know she and Guy had had dinner, not only from the dishes but from the two chops that were gone. That was okay, she could explain that. What she could not explain was that her love for Wallace was no longer there, and through no fault of his own.

Nora was in bed when he came home, and she feigned sleep, hearing him downstairs, and then later sliding into bed next to her, the sound of his shirt landing on the floor. She stayed that way until he fell asleep, and she could smell the alcohol on him, and she lay with the knowledge that rest would elude her this night. She turned on her side and looked out the open window, down to the lake, barely visible in the moonless night, and she realized that she had taken a step this evening that would take her to new places, places she had never gone, places she had never intended to go. In the span of a few hours, everything had changed. She needed time to think, to digest what it all meant. But that would come later. For now her mind was filled with thoughts of their lovemaking and of tomorrow, when she would see him again. She wondered how much of it would show on her face.

12

It was several weeks after our trip to visit Nora that I again saw Wallace. In truth, I was doing what I often do when I fear conflict: avoiding it. In fact, I had done it with this man before, after I had seen him praying at the base of the apple tree on the high pasture above his house. This time was different, though, for then my transgression was an accident, a case of being in the wrong place at the wrong time, not a betrayal. Though as Kate pointed out, it was Wallace's lie that led to it. I did not know how to reconcile that with my decision to travel to the Adirondacks, so for several weeks I didn't, and avoided Wallace, which of course he noticed: at the very least, he was perceptive. It was unlike me to disappear for weeks, unless something was going on. Sooner or later I knew I had to face him, though I put it off for as long as I could.

One afternoon during those two weeks an ice storm hit. While snow had little effect in Eden, ice was a different matter. Everything shut down, and even the post office was not immune. Connie had been listening to the weather on the radio all day, and when the sky started to spit ice, falling in small lumps, clinging to trees and power lines, she sent me home.

I drove carefully, and the ice was falling hard, looking like rain except where it hit the ground, and soon the roads were as slick as skating rinks, but I took it slow and I was the only car out and I made it home.

In my driveway I was pleased to see Kate's pickup truck and even more pleased to see her inside, sitting at my kitchen table drinking tea and aimlessly flipping through the pages of a magazine.

'I thought you might want some company,' she said. 'They said it's going to be a long one.'

Soon it grew dark, and we made a simple dinner of salad and pasta and drank wine, and outside we could hear the wind picking up, rattling the windows in my small cabin, and shortly after that the power went out, and I lit candles, and after dinner Kate and I lay on the couch and we spooned. There was the light from the candles and the light from the fire in the woodstove and the sound of the wind, but other than that the only thing I could hear was our breathing. Eventually we fell asleep like that, and when I woke in the middle of the night one of the candles had burned out and the other was about to, and the fire in the woodstove glowed dimly. Outside I could hear the ice falling, but I could not see anything, and I wondered what it would look like in the morning.

I quietly extricated myself from Kate on the couch and stood and went to the woodstove, opened the door, and with the poker reached in and stoked the coals. From behind the stove I grabbed two ash logs and put them into the box, watched as the flames from the coals began to lick up their sides, and waited until they started to catch before I closed the door.

When I turned back around, Kate was lying on the couch with her eyes open, and she looked sleepy and beautiful, and she opened her arms toward the ceiling for me to hug her, and I went to her and took her embrace, and I rolled into her, and she into me, and in the diminishing light of the candle and growing light of the stove, we slowly undressed each other and then we made love.

After, as Kate lay with her head in the space where my shoulder meets my arm, I felt a warmth I did not think possible, and when I looked down I saw that her eyes were open, and she saw me looking at her and she smiled and she ran a hand across my chest. I took the arm that she was not lying on and ran that hand through her hair, and she sighed as I did so, and then, before the rush of fear and sensibleness could take over and stop me, I asked Kate to marry me.

'Kate,' I said, 'I want to spend my life with you.'

She looked up at me. 'What do you mean?'

'I want you to be my wife, I want you to marry me.'

'Are you asking me or telling me?'

'I'm asking you.'

'Then ask.'

I slid off the couch, and got on one knee in front of the

couch, and Kate rolled over so that she faced me. Her eyes looked bright in the half-dark, and our faces were only inches apart.

'Will you marry me?' I said.

Kate looked at me for a long moment. 'I don't think so, Nathan,' she said.

'What do you mean?' I said.

'I don't know,' she said, reaching over and brushing my hair away from my forehead. 'I'm not really sure that you love me.'

This irritated me. 'Of course I love you. Jesus, I'm asking you to marry me.'

'No,' said Kate, 'I think you love the idea of me.'

'And what would that be?'

She paused, glanced over my head toward one of the windows that in the daytime looked up the land to the road. 'That I'm young. I'm here. Available to you. I don't get in the way. You say I'm beautiful, but sometimes I catch you looking at me and I know you are looking for flaws, and I have many. I can see your brain trying to figure out how I might age, and whether or not you'll still be attracted to me. I see you look at other women when we're in town, and I know that some-where inside you are always wondering if the real one for you is out there and you just haven't met her yet. And all that's okay, Nathan, 'cause that is the way you are and I accept it and I love you anyway. But until you reach that place where you can fully *be* with me, where it is me and only me, where if I lost all my hair and my breasts sagged to my waist you would still think I was the most beautiful woman you'd ever seen, then I can't, I won't, marry you.'

When Kate finished she smiled at me and again brushed my hair away from my forehead.

'Kate,' I said, 'I really really love you. And I mean that. So some of the things you said might be true, I can't help it. But that doesn't change the fact that I love you. More than I have loved anything in my life. And that truth should be stronger than all others.'

'Come to bed, Nathan,' Kate said. 'It's really late. We can talk about this tomorrow.'

And I did as she said, I went to bed, and together we lay while outside the ice continued to fall, and in the morning the world was transformed, giant pine trees bent almost to the ground and heavy with ice, the sky gray and the forests bright with gray light, ice piled on the porch and as far as the eye could see, while inside the world had been transformed as well: I had asked Kate to marry me in the middle of the night, and already it felt like another life, like it had happened to someone else, but the truth was I had taken that step and been rebuffed, and now both of us had to move forward as if it did not weigh between us, which in hindsight it did not for, as with most things with Kate, she shrugged it off, and it was my cross to bear alone.

FOR TWO days the town worked on cleaning roads of fallen trees and sanding the icy roads while the power company brought back downed lines and, hill by hill, the town of Eden woke up again. Kate and I spent these two days frozen in time, sleeping late in front of the woodstove, playing Scrabble, drinking wine, and eating what little food there was in the house. It would have been one of those times I would have cherished if it were not for the gulf I felt because of her rejection, and when on the third day the weather suddenly warmed and the sun came through the gunmetal gray sky and the power returned, I was happy to be back at work, doing my route.

Now that I was out of the cabin, my thoughts once again were about Wallace. I knew I needed to go by there, and I felt an overwhelming urge to confess to our trip to New York, but I was scared, too, the way you are when you know you need to tell a friend something you wish you didn't. When I went by his house delivering the mail, I did not see him, though the lamp was lit in the downstairs window, and I figured he was where he always was when he was not working, sitting in his chair, looking out the window at the frozen lake, alone with his thoughts, his memories.

After work I stopped by the liquor store, and the small town was full of people, all of us having been released at once from our icy prisons. I bought a bottle of scotch, a better one than we usually drank, a single malt that cost me thirty dollars, and then I drove the familiar roads to Mirror Lake, marveling as I did doing my route at the extent of the damage from the storm, whole swatches of forest brought down under its oppressive weight, men in jumpsuits with chain saws seemingly working around every bend.

When I knocked on Wallace's door I did not hear anything, so I opened it and called his name. I then heard his gruff voice, and when I walked through the kitchen and into his living room, there he was in the chair, and he rubbed his eyes when he saw me.

'I was sleeping,' he said.

'You want me to come back?'

'No, no, come in.'

I sat down on the couch next to him, and it was warm in there, the woodstove was kicking hard, and I took off my coat. Wallace stood and lit another oil lamp on the table next to me and it brightened the room, and I realized in that moment that he had been living in just this one room. His clothes were slung over a wooden chair, and his pillows and bedding were on the floor. I wondered why he had shrunk his world this way but I did not ask. I removed the single malt scotch from the brown bag and held it up to the light, and Wallace saw it and came and took it from my hands.

'Look at this,' he said. 'I always knew you were a good man, Nathan.'

'The good stuff,' I said.

'What, did you get engaged or something?'

'No.' I laughed. 'She said no.'

'Sensible girl, that Kate.'

Wallace went to the kitchen and returned with two small glasses, put them down on the coffee table, and then cracked the seal on the scotch and poured two fingers for each of us. When he handed me the glass I tasted it, and the extra twenty bucks really made a difference, for the scotch was peaty and rich and had a deep flavor and it lingered in your mouth for what seemed like an eternity after you swallowed it.

'Damn that's good,' Wallace said.

I nodded and looked at him, and he looked rough and old to me, as if the several weeks I hadn't seen him had taken a toll. I got the sense that perhaps he had been drinking more than usual, or maybe it was just the reality of the ice storm, keeping him inside, which for Wallace was the equivalent of being put into a cage. I thought for a moment about putting off why I was here, but I could not, there was the expensive scotch which I had bought, but more important there was the reality of my guilt at having seen Nora, which frankly had taken a backseat in recent days to my failed attempt to ask for Kate's hand.

'Wallace,' I said. 'I have something to tell you.'

He lowered his eyes, looked at me. 'Shoot.'

'I saw Nora.'

He nodded, looked away. 'So?'

'I know she's alive.'

Wallace looked away from me, over my head to the darkness outside. I saw him biting his lip, and then he turned quickly back to me, and in his voice I could hear traces of anger, as if he was trying not to lose control. I was undeterred.

He said, 'What do you want from me?'

'The truth.'

'What truth?'

'The truth about you and Nora.'

'Everything I told you has been true.'

'Except you said that she was dead.'

'Yes,' he said, 'except I said that she was dead.'

'I know it should be none of my business, and if that's the way you want it, fine. It's just that you made it my business, with your stories.'

'That didn't give you the right to go there.'

'I know. I couldn't help it. Not that that's an excuse, it's not. I had to know if it was the same Nora Fiske.'

I explained to Wallace how I had discovered it, the errant letter, and while I did I looked around the living room, and it was simply that with the ice storm it had become Wallace's prison cell, and it reflected that. Or perhaps it was just that it was dark in here, dark outside, and the shortness of the days in a Vermont winter had begun to filter into my perspective. Either way, I told Wallace the story of our trip to Jay, New York, and I told him parts of our conversation with Nora, though I did not tell him what she had said about Guy; he would have to tell me that if he knew it, for though I felt bold with my glass of single malt in my hand, I knew enough to know that you don't tell a man directly that his wife had an affair, even if it was forty years ago and the man is now in his late seventies.

But then when I finished my story and took a long sip of scotch, I saw that Wallace was staring once again out the window, like a man about to measure his words. I watched as his eyes narrowed when he turned them to me and said, 'What did she say about Guy?'

I shrugged. 'Not much.'

'How can you expect the truth from me if you won't give it yourself?'

I sighed. 'Wallace –'

'Say it, Nathan. I can take it.'

So I told him, my eyes on my feet, aware that my voice quaked a little while I spoke, and I told him what I knew, about their first time together, about how it happened that summer when she miscarried, about how she did not intend it to happen but that she fell in love with him, much as she had fallen in love with Wallace before, and I told him what she told me about that first night together, when they swam in the lake while he was in Montpelier, and then I told him that she said he was the love of her life. And I hated myself for saying it, because I would hate to have it said to me, and I could only imagine what it felt like, to know that your wife slept with another man on the lawn in front of the house you shared, and the man was a friend and someone you trusted.

I have lost my parents and grieved for that, and the grief is heady and strong, but you know that grief will heal someday, for there is nothing you can do about death; death happens to all of us eventually and, while maybe we could live differently to postpone it, the simple fact is that people come and go, and what matters is how much you loved them while they were around. No regrets. But I have never had to grieve for a love lost in the arms of another, and I can only think that it hurts, hurts like hell, like a kick in the balls that stays with you forever. For once it happens you can never change it, and it must color the entirety of the relationship, not just from the moment of the betrayal forward, but all of it: calls it into question, makes you wonder whether the early love and passion you had was even real.

No: I cannot imagine that. But Wallace not only had to imagine it, he had to live it, and my only relief in telling him was the realization that I wasn't telling him anything he did not know already. It was clear from his face that he knew all of it, and much more, in fact. I was simply summarizing a piece of it for him, what I learned from Nora, saving him the time, as it turned out, of telling me himself.

AFTER I talked Wallace did not say anything. He filled his pipe, lit it, and I took his lighter out of his hands and lit a cigarette. My hands shook as I brought it to my mouth, inhaled.

I finally spoke. I said, 'I'm really sorry, Wallace. I shouldn't have gone there.'

'Ah, fuck it,' he said. 'You know what you know.'

'I just thought. I don't know. I don't know what I thought.'

'You thought you were going to figure something out is what you thought. You thought you'd understand something you could use yourself. Well, it doesn't work that way. I was not the first guy who had his wife cheat on him, and I won't be the last. It happens all the time. And my experience was long ago, and it happened, there's no getting around that. But you can't take what you know and pretend to understand about everything from it. My situation was my situation and that's it. Everyone is different. What happened between Nora and me was different. It belonged to us. Not to you, not to Kate.'

'That's not what I thought,' I said.

'You know what, Nathan?' Wallace said. 'I don't give a shit.'

And then Wallace turned back to his pipe, and to his scotch, and we sat in silence. I listened to the ticking of the wood-stove, smoked a cigarette, lit another, smoked that, too. I looked at Wallace, who would not catch my eye; I looked at his wrinkled face, his red eyes, his prominent forehead; I looked at his hands, one resting in his lap, curled around the glass of scotch, the other in the air in front of his face, holding the pipe stem. They were old hands, with loose skin and large veins. But they were strong hands, too, the hands of a man who had spent his whole life working, and I thought then how different we were, that we had somehow become friends and I had put so much weight on his story, and he was right, I did want to appropriate it, to apply it to myself, and perhaps you could not take the specific and make it universal like that. Maybe that was too much to ask.

We sat in silence until Wallace dozed off and, when he did, I took the pipe from his hand, emptied its contents into the ashtray, and took the glass of scotch from his hand and put it on the table. Then I put another log in the woodstove and turned down the dampers. I found a blanket from behind Wallace's chair, and I wrapped it over him. I blew out the oil lamps and, with only the light from the woodstove, I found my way to the door and out to the Jeep.

When I got home I was suddenly incredibly tired and drained, and I just wanted to climb into bed and sleep deeply when Kate called to tell me she wanted to take a break. She said she thought we would benefit from the time apart, but I thought this could mean only one thing: the end of us.

I said, 'I want to see you.'

'Not now, Nathan. In a week. Let's just take a week and be apart and see how it feels.'

'I'll never see you again if that happens.'

'Don't be dramatic. I'm not going anywhere; you're not going anywhere. One week.'

And so we did, took a week off in the middle of winter, and I felt loosed from my moorings and alone, and every day after work I wanted to pick up the phone and call her, and sometimes I did, picked it up, even started dialing, before I put it back in its cradle. Instead what I did was drive the back roads of Eden, drinking wine out of the bottle and smoking cigarettes, doing loops past the house which Kate shared with Linger, and I was pleased to see her truck there, for it meant that she was staying home, and not seeing someone else.

At night I slept like shit, and some nights I'd roll over and expect to run into her. I could have rolled right off the bed and onto the floor. I needed her, I knew that; and Kate might say it was only the idea of her I needed, but on those long winter nights when I lay in bed alone I knew that was bull-shit; I knew that the idea of her didn't do me a damn bit of good; I couldn't wrap my arms around it, I couldn't make love to it, I couldn't wake up next to it with any certainty at all. No: what I needed was Kate, pure and simple, beautiful, tangible Kate; Kate with the mousy hair and the common sense, Kate with the turquoise eyes that kept me grounded.

It was a long week, and I did my part, though I longed to hear the phone ring and her voice on the other end of the line or, better yet, to hear a knock at the door and see her there, and one night while it snowed hard outside I was climbing into bed when I heard the knock I had been waiting for, and I practically ran downstairs to get it, ready to take her into my arms and pick up where we left off. Instead, it was

Wallace I saw, snow in his hair and hanging from his thick eyebrows, and he wore no coat, only a flannel shirt and jeans, and in one hand he carried the bottle of single malt I had left with him, and he had not finished it but saved it for us to drink together, which pleased me, and which we did that night, while a heavy snow fell, drank the good peaty scotch in front of the woodstove, and this time I listened while Wallace continued his story, trying as hard as I could not to take solace in his pain as a way to relieve my own.

13

Some nights sleeping with Wallace, Nora felt him reach for her, and she would feel his hands on her back and then her sides, pulling her to him, and on those nights she would try to shrug him off as if she were too tired, pushing his hands away, but some nights, too, he persisted and she gave in, for she was his wife, and when he moved above her she closed her eyes and imagined Guy, and she knew that this betrayal was in some ways worse than the actual physical one, but she did not know any way around it. This was in October. The nights were cool and the days warm and, lying there after he had finished, Nora would look out the window to Mirror Lake, and listen while Wallace snored, and while the lake was shimmering and beautiful in the moonlight, she found herself wishing that their bedroom looked out onto the back of the house, toward the barn, so that she could at least see the light in Guy's window, know that he was there in his own bed, thinking on her the way she thought on him.

Some nights, as well, Wallace drank more than usual, and these were the nights she looked forward to, for he would sleep soundly if fitfully, and she would wait next to him until his snoring developed a rhythm, and then she would make her way out of the house and across the field to Guy. When she climbed the ladder to his room, he was always there, extending his hand down to her, helping her up, taking her in his arms when her feet were firmly on the floorboards, and sometimes they would make love right away, as if they could not keep apart, mad for each other; and sometimes they would sit and talk and he would hold her. Nora loved when he lay behind her and held her, and she was afraid of sleep because she did not want to miss this time, the consciousness of their presence together, its preciousness, and while they lay in silence, no need for words, she would watch the gradual lightening of the sky, its shades moving from black to blue before she rose and returned to the house.

One night after they made love she got to her feet and went to the window, and outside the night was moonless, and with the lights out in the room she could see the stars, millions of them, and in the pasture below she could make out the Jerseys and she could see the shadow that was the house she shared with Wallace. Turning back around, she saw Guy's face appear for a moment as he lit his cigarette, and she saw his chest and his arms that had just held her. She stood naked in the window until he said, 'What are you looking for out there?'

'I don't know,' said Nora.

'Come to bed.'

'I should go.'

'We have a few hours, come to bed.'

Nora went to him, and he stubbed his cigarette out in the ashtray on the chair next to his bed. She sat down on the edge of the bed and put her hand on his thigh.

'I don't know if we can keep doing this,' she said.

'It's not something we can choose.'

'Of course it is. I'm married, Guy.'

'You should be with me, you know that.'

She looked toward his face, and she wished the light were on so she could see his eyes. 'I wish it were so easy.'

'It could be,' said Guy.

'How?'

'Leave him.'

'I can't do that.'

'Bullshit. I don't like you having to go back there, I don't like him touching you. It doesn't make sense. You love me and yet you lay in bed with him and you let him inside you. That's not right, Nora. You have to know that.'

Nora looked across the dark room at the window. She felt tears in her eyes, and she was grateful for the dark because Guy had not seen her this way and she did not want him to see her this way. She loved Guy, she knew that; she loved him like she had never loved Wallace, like she never would love Wallace. There were times when she and Wallace were first together that she felt something she thought was love, but it was different. It was comfort and ease and the promise of a life together. When Wallace looked on her in those days she felt a warmth, and she felt his desire to possess her, but it was a different desire, the desire that comes when a man finds a woman who he thinks will make a good wife.

It was a practical life, and their coming together made sense. And for many women, she thought, that should be enough, for finding someone you can spend your life with, share the work with, grow old together and all that, was an accomplishment. When Guy looked on her, it was his desire she felt, too, but it was different. It was passion and lust, and part of her wanted to stay away from him, knowing that she was jeopardizing everything she had, but a bigger part of her knew that giving in was the least she could do, was the only thing you can do, for once you get it in your head you are halfway there, and all that is left is the consummation, the act itself.

That night when she returned to the house, a front had moved in, and the sky was split in two, the clear blue of early dawn above her, and over the lake there was a bank of clouds, thick and black, and it was these she watched as she walked, oblivious to the cows that she walked past, the cool earth beneath her feet, oblivious even to the figure of Wallace in the yard, his back to her, his hands on his hips, facing Mirror Lake.

By the time Nora saw him it was too late, and she kept walking, concentrating on her footing, one in front of the other, aware of the beating of her heart. When he heard her footsteps he turned, looked at her, and she felt his eyes on her, on her face, then her bare legs, and she wondered if he knew, what she would say if he did. Then just as quickly he turned back to the lake, and she went to him, stood next to him, and she followed his eyes to the gray water, the coming storm already blowing the surface into a light chop.

'I couldn't sleep,' she said.

Wallace nodded. 'Going to be some storm,' he said.

'Are you up for good?'

'I think so.'

Nora put her arm around him, moved into him, and she felt him stiffen, and at that moment she felt the first of the cold rain on her arms, and yet she stood her ground, and his arm came around her, and soon it was raining hard, cool October rain, wet on her face, her arms, her legs, and she stayed until his arm came off her, and then she watched him head toward the barn and to Guy, to the morning's work, and she went into the house and the bed he had left, and while she lay there knowing the two of them were working together, she vowed to end it no matter how difficult, to return to what she had built with Wallace, even though she now knew what love felt like.

THE LAST week of October the Indian summer came and the days were very warm, in the eighties, and it lifted Nora's spirits to have this sudden blast of heat when the leaves were already off the trees. She had grown more careful in her dalliances with Guy, and she found herself moving warily around Wallace, like a cat, and sometimes when she thought about it she realized that she was not being true to either man or, more important, to herself. But those times were rare, and mostly she felt like she had reached some sort of equilibrium, and she tried not to think about what it all meant, for if she were to she would realize the ephemeral nature of it all, and would know that it would not last, could not last, this way.

And so she developed a curious distance from it, sharing a bed with Wallace at night, finding time to sneak away to the barn to be with Guy, surreptitiously making her way back to the house after, hoping not to run into him again. And then, during the days, it was as if everything were whole again, as if nothing had ever happened, and she did her part of the farm-work and Wallace and Guy did theirs; and it was only at night that the complexity of her choices took form and shape, yet she had grown numb to them: they were no more present to her than the mist that rose off the fields on those late fall mornings.

One afternoon Wallace had gone to town and Nora was upstairs in their bedroom folding laundry when she heard foot-steps on the stairs, and she turned and looked and it was Guy, and he came into the room and before she could say anything he was behind her, with his arms around her, and she tried to pull his arms away but he did not let them go.

'Guy,' she said, 'you can't be up here.'

'I want to make love in his bed.'

Nora tried to keep her voice calm. 'No,' she said. 'We can't.'

But she felt Guy kissing the back of her neck and his voice whispering in her ear, 'I know you want to,' and she shook her head and said no, but her resolve was escaping her, and when he pushed her into the side of the bed and then on top of it, she did not resist; and when he took her dress up over her head, she did not resist; and soon he was inside her and she lay and looked at the ceiling as she had when Wallace had been where Guy was, and she looked out the window to the lake and the road that ran alongside it; and then she closed her eyes and tried to enjoy it, the feel of him, but she could not.

When he had finished and rolled off of her, lay next to her with his breaths coming fast and hard from the exertion, she fought the urge to fall asleep, to close her eyes and wish this away. She said, 'I don't like the way you make me feel anymore.'

Guy leaned up on his elbows. 'I don't understand.'

'You have no sympathy for me. You say you do, but you don't. You come up here and you fuck me in my husband's bed. It's my fault, too, I gave in to it, but that shouldn't matter. Some things should belong only to Wallace. It's one thing to fuck another man's wife. It's a whole other thing to fuck his wife in his own bed.'

Guy laughed. 'I like it when you get angry, Nora. I really do. It shows you're alive.'

'You can be a bastard, you know that?'

'Because I fuck you in your husband's bed? Is that why? Well, your husband doesn't deserve this bed, and he doesn't deserve to have you in it. We love each other, no? No? Answer me.'

Nora looked up at him, at his narrow black eyes, two days' worth of growth on his chin. 'Yes,' she said.

'Yes,' said Guy. 'And if we love each other, then where we fuck is our business.'

Nora closed her eyes. She saw colors against her lids, reds

and blues and bright yellows. She opened them and rolled away from Guy, and out the window she could see the bright sun reflecting off the stillness of the lake, and the water was a dark, dark blue, and beyond that she could see the leafless trees on the opposite shore, gold in the afternoon light. 'You need to leave now,' she said.

She heard him rising behind her, and he stopped and leaned over her and kissed her forcefully on her upraised cheek next to her mouth, before continuing on up. She heard his feet on the floor, and then the buckle of his belt being refastened, and then, 'Okay, I go.'

And she was grateful for the space alone, and she lay looking out at the lake, and soon she saw dirt rising on the road before the bend by the water, and then she saw Wallace's truck, black and sluggish, and she heard him shifting the gears for the final half mile of hill, and by the time he pulled in she had straightened the bed and was back folding the laundry, as if she had been doing it all along.

THAT NIGHT when Wallace returned from stacking wood, Nora greeted him at the door in a blue sundress that brought out the color of her hair, of her eyes. She had not worn it since before they were married, when they courted, when he used to walk her home from the schoolhouse. She had a glass of whiskey for him, and she drew him a bath, and he did not ask her why she was acting this way, and she did not offer an explanation. While he bathed she sat in a chair next to the tub, and from time to time she took the wet cloth off the tub's edge and rubbed it with soap, then wrung it out onto his arms, the soap running off his biceps and into the water, and then she washed him, his arms, his chest, his face. And when he grew aroused she playfully reached down for it, and he smiled at her, and when his drink was finished she replenished it.

After, while he dressed, she fried the good tenderloin of steak in a pan with onions and peppers and made a salad of greens, and they ate at the table in the kitchen under the flickering shadows of candlelight. They talked about general things while they ate, the work he had done that day, the work in front of him, the recent warm weather, what it meant. They did not talk about each other, though Nora knew that Wallace knew that she was reaching out, and their silence about it was a tacit acknowledgment of its existence, and neither of them wanted to make it disappear by giving it words.

After dinner Nora led him to the couch, and she undressed him in the dark, and then she went to him and she took him in her mouth, something she had not done for a long time, and while she moved over him he ran his hands through her hair and he asked her to come up but she refused and instead finished him that way, knowing that he liked it.

In bed that night she lay in the crook of his arm, and in the unusual late fall warmth, he said to her, 'I'm glad you're back.'

'I didn't know I left.'

'Yes,' Wallace said, 'you did.'

And that is all she said, and all he said, and when his breathing steadied and she knew he was asleep, she thought that maybe he was right, that she was back, that she could be back, and it felt good thinking that, but somewhere inside her she knew it was not completely true, that out in the barn she had another life, one that lured her away, its pull stronger than she could fully understand.

14

There are times even now when I do not see what Kate saw in me, when I think I had been true and strong and shown her everything I had. There are times when I think that I had finally turned a corner with her, that she was different, she was the one, the one who could pull me out of my fears, drag me into something deeper. But if I learned anything about myself during that long Vermont winter when things seemed to be slipping away from us, I learned that I am a difficult man to love; that I have good qualities, sure, a naïve romanticism for one; but that by and large I am hard to ever truly know, and being in love with me requires patience and a willingness to tolerate my need to push away at the same time I pull close; to live with a degree of ambiguity; and, most of all, a willingness to find within yourself the strength that I seem incapable of fully providing.

We had been apart for a week and, when it ended, I suppose I thought we would instantly be back into it. As if the week came to an end at an appointed time and she would simply reappear and things would be as they were. Of course, it did not work that way.

It was actually eight days, not seven, before I saw her again. It was a clear and cool January afternoon, and the sky was the palest of blues, cloudless, and the sun off the snow was almost blinding. I hurried through my route, thinking of her all day, wanting to stop early and go by her place.

Then, when I had delivered the last pieces of mail, I stopped at a store and picked up some beer, parked on a side road about a mile away from the apartment above the bar Kate shared with Linger. Sitting there, I rapidly drank two beers and chain-smoked cigarettes, watched cars go by on the snow-covered road, and built up my courage to see her. I was more nervous than if it were our first date, and I wondered how she would react to me. Would she be happy to see me, as I hoped? Would she say we had to talk, then proceed to end it forever? Or, worst-case scenario: would she tell me she had fallen for someone else?

At the door to her apartment I could see the television on, and when I knocked it was Linger who answered.

'Hey, Nathan,' he said.

'Linger. Is Kate here?'

'She ran to the store. She should be back. You can wait for her if you want.'

'I'd like that.'

Inside I sat on the couch in the dark living room and Linger sat in his chair, a full ashtray on the arm, can of Coke in his hand. The television was tuned to a daytime talk show, and I did not recognize the host, a thin blond woman in a red power suit. Onstage were two couples, and the women were shouting at each other. Apparently, each had been married to the other's husband, and now they lived next to one another and were full of hate, at least enough to go on television, and talk about.

'You think we got problems,' Linger said. 'Jeezum Crow.'

I laughed. 'How can you watch this shit?'

'You should try it. It'll make you feel better. Guaranteed.'

I sank into the couch and looked around the room. I had been in here before, but only briefly. The room was small and organized around the television, which was large and sat in the center. It reeked of stale cigarettes. Besides Linger's chair and this couch, there was a short pine bookcase, and above it on the wall was a painting of a bridge with mountains behind it. Next to the bookcase was an end table that displayed photographs: Kate's high school photo, a picture of Linger as a young man in shorts on the beach, and then a picture of Kate's mother, who was blond like Kate and had her green eyes. She had died of breast cancer when Kate was twelve and, like me with my mother, Kate never talked about her.

It was only a few minutes after that that I heard the front door, and Linger said, 'Here she is,' and then there she was, in the room, and having not seen her in eight days she looked different to me, more beautiful if that were possible, but different: it was as if I were seeing her for the first time, but that was not it either; she was not a stranger; she was the Kate I knew, only I was seeing her with fresh, if educated, eyes; and it took every ounce of will I possessed not to run to her and take her out of this sad, little apartment, out of this life.

'Hi, Kate,' I said when she saw me.

She smiled. 'Nathan. Has it really been a week?'

And I knew then that she was mocking me, but it was okay, it was good, in fact, this was definitely the Kate I knew, the one I loved, the woman who could cut me to size in a minute only to build me back up the next.

She nodded to Linger. 'Hi, Daddy.'

'Hey, baby,' he said, his voice throaty with cigarettes. 'You two want to be alone?'

'No,' said Kate. 'We're leaving.'

And we did, we left, like we had plans, and in the Jeep we spoke only enough to decide where to go, and I drove in silence down the darkening roads, nightfall coming quick in the winter sky, and I drove us to a restaurant in St J. we had been to before, a little café with a bar you could eat at.

At the bar we ordered wine and hamburgers and fries and she sat close to me and all I could do was look at her. I looked at her hair, her wispy hair, at her eyes, those turquoise eyes. I looked at her thin, wiry arms. I looked at her breasts beneath her shirt. And mostly I looked at her face, for it was her face that I loved the most, plain perhaps if you didn't know her, but beautiful to me.

'Are you going to just stare at me?' she said.

'I missed you.'

'I missed you, too.'

'For real? You did?'

'What do you think? Of course I did, Nathan.'

'I don't want to do that again.'

'Do what?'

'Have you gone for a week.'

The bartender brought us the wine, and we stopped talking long enough to sip from our glasses.

'I think it was good, Nathan, I really do,' Kate said.

'I love you, Kate.'

'I know.'

'Do you love me?'

'It's hard for me, Nathan. I want to love you, you need to know that.'

'That's not enough for me,' I said. 'I mean, I'll take what I can get.'

Kate nodded. 'I know,' she said, and then she breathed deep. 'This is hard.'

'Are you breaking up with me?'

Kate looked away, at the bartender, who was pretending to be busy folding napkins. And then, much to my relief, she said, 'No, I don't think so.'

I reached my hand out and took her chin in it, turned her face to me. 'I want you to come home with me tonight, Kate,' I said.

'I don't know that that would solve anything.'

'It doesn't have to.'

'That's what I'm afraid of,' Kate said.

This made me angry. 'What exactly are we trying to solve? It would help me a lot if I knew that.'

'Why do you love me, Nathan?'

And so I told her. I told her how she consumed me, how it just, for lack of better language, felt right. I told her how I loved the way she looked in the morning, her hair a mess, lines from the pillow on her face. I told her how I loved how she didn't take any of my shit. I told her how I admired her strength, her pride. How she grew up in a bar and was never for a minute ashamed of it. I told her that I did not think of other women when I was with her; that I did not even so much as look at other women, and how this was different from my past experiences. I told her that I was not in love with the idea of her, as she imagined, that I loved her, her flesh, her mind, the very essence of her. I told her that I was young and stupid and did not know much but one thing I knew with absolute certainty was that I needed her, and that I knew that this was not simply a passing fantasy but it was everything. I said, 'Without you, Kate, there is just me. And that doesn't cut it. With you, I have everything.'

When I finished, her eyes were wet and she said nothing, so I said, 'Give us a chance, Kate. Give us a chance.'

She paused and looked me right in the eyes. Then she said what I wanted her to say. She said, 'Okay, Nathan,' and she reached out and placed her hand on mine.

The bartender brought us our hamburgers and fries, and it was hardly a memorable meal but sustenance nonetheless, which was all I needed that night, some food to temper the alcohol, some food to ground us in something more concrete than my words.

After, we drove the dark snowy roads back to Eden and we

shared a cigarette as we went, and at one point we rounded a tight bend in the road and a vista of open fields and mountains greeted us in the blue dark, the moonlight playing off the snow and lighting up the world.

'Stop here,' said Kate.

'Why?'

'Trust me.'

So I did as she said, pulled the Jeep over on the side of the road, and we both got out. The night was cold but after the food and the wine did not feel so bad. To our left was a small farmhouse, all the lights off, a Volvo in the driveway. To our right were open fields, woods visible at their perimeter. The sky was a deep blue, and the gibbous moon sat above the trees. There were no stars.

To my surprise, Kate began to walk across the field toward the woods.

'Where are you going?'

'Follow me, Nathan, you'll see.'

As soon as I left the road I realized we were on a trail, probably for cross-country skiing, as the snow beneath our feet was hard-packed and easy to walk on, while on either side of us it was deep enough to require snowshoes. I walked behind Kate and we made good time across the field and I knew then that she was heading for the woods, though I did not know why. The night was silent and still, the only sound coming from the crunching of packed snow under our boots.

Kate reached the woods first and quickly vanished into the trees and I had a moment of panic before I entered too and could see her again, her body silhouetted by the moonlight coming through the treetops. The path narrowed and the trees were on either side of us now, closer, and it was darker in here than it was in the field, but my eyes adjusted nicely and I followed several feet behind her. In no time we were climbing on the path, and then it opened a little bit and I realized we were following a ridgeline. The trees were larger here, ash mostly it looked like, and I moved carefully, listening for sounds, for animals.

We walked like this for fifteen minutes, along the spine of this unnamed hill, and it led us through a monotony of deep woods, and I wanted to ask Kate where we were going, why this nighttime hike, but I knew she liked the mystery of it all and I let her have it.

Then, just when I was losing my patience and about to shatter the silence with a question, Kate stopped in front of me and turned to face me.

'Okay,' she said. 'We're here.'

'Where?'

'You'll see.'

She walked forward and I watched her move between two large trees and a few feet down a small hill. I waited until I saw her stop again and then I joined her and I knew in that instant what it was she'd brought me to see. In front of us was a snow-covered mountain lake, small and surrounded by stark ridges, the moonlight sweeping across its surface. There were no houses and, from the looks of it, we had taken the only way to it. It was one of the most beautiful things I have ever seen, and if it were not for the well-groomed trail that led us

to it, I would have thought that we were the first people ever
to set eyes on it.

'What do you think?' Kate said.

'It's amazing. What's it called?'

'Mirror Lake.'

I laughed. 'You're kidding. That's the name of Wallace's
pond.'

'He didn't copyright it, Nathan.'

'I know. But still. Two Mirror Lakes in the same town?
What are the odds of that?'

'This one isn't even on the maps,' Kate said. 'Not that people
don't know about it. Some do. My father took me here when
I was a little girl, and at least once a year I try to walk back
here, see it again.'

'It's perfect,' I said.

And I stood there staring at it, this hidden mountain lake
in the woods, and after a few minutes Kate broke into a run
and went onto the ice, which scared the hell out of me, for
in my mind's eye I saw her falling through and me failing to
rescue her.

'Kate, get off of there,' I said.

'Come on, Nathan,' she said. 'You have to stand in the
middle.'

And so I swallowed my fear, ran after her, the snow deep
on the ice, and out in the middle of the lake we could look
at the sky like it was ours alone, and the mountain ridges
leaned in toward us and the forest did, too, and I decided in
that moment that this Mirror Lake belonged to nobody but
Kate and me and, standing on ice that felt as firm as hard

earth, I picked her up in my arms and she whooped as I did, her voice echoing off the hills, returning only to me.

THAT NIGHT, while Kate snored softly next to me, I looked out the window and watched the humpbacked moon over the trees and I thought about Mirror Lake. Of course I should have known that Wallace's was not the only one in the world, but the idea that there was one so close, and hidden, and different, had an effect on me. I suppose I realized that Wallace's story did not have to be my own, that if he had his lake, then goddamn it, I would have mine. And I don't know if Kate knew this and did it consciously to wake me up to something beyond the story I had been living. In hindsight, I like to think that she did. That she had that kind of prescience.

I slept fitfully that night, and in the morning I was deliciously tired and rolled into Kate and held her until she woke. I had an hour before I needed to be at the post office, and we made love, like we used to, and it was passionate and easy and afterward we showered together and I remember thinking while the water ran over both of us that I could never let her down again, that I needed to change my ways, whatever they were; that I needed to do whatever it took to keep her in my life.

In the weeks that followed Kate and I moved back toward each other, imperfectly, yes, but back toward each other. It was a fragile bond we had, one that needed a lot of attention, and I did my best to give it that. Soon it would be spring, and the ice and snow would melt, and the rivers would run high, and the world would turn instantly and shockingly green, until the only reminder of winter was a thin membrane of ice on Mirror Lakes everywhere. Our job in that time was to watch that melt, too.

15

There were things that came together for Wallace after the fact, the way that stories often do, and when he looked back on it years later he saw it all laid in front of him, and he knew he should have seen the obvious before it affected him directly. First, there was the miscarriage, and his failure to recognize that for what it was, to try to find a way to close the gulf that had opened between them. Then there were the various hints, things Guy said, things Nora said, small comments, really, but enough that in hindsight it seemed should have shown him the truth of their relationship. And there was that October night when he awoke to find her gone, half past four on the clock, and he rose and went downstairs and did not find her there either, and looked outside and wondered where she was. Then, standing on the lawn, looking out over the lake, he felt her presence before he saw her, and then she was behind him, and when he turned and saw her nightdress and her bare legs, her mud boots, he should have known that something was amiss.

But the truth of it all was that Wallace trusted her implicitly; and he trusted Guy, too; and though he knew that since the miscarriage, and perhaps even before, things had changed between them, he also knew that his feelings for her remained whole and unadulterated; and if he was guilty of anything it was assuming that Nora would react and feel precisely as he did; that they were two parts of the same organism, perhaps drifting away a bit, but never losing sight of what it was that held them together.

In the depth of winter, though, Wallace thought whatever they had lost that summer day when he wrapped their son in a blanket and laid him under a tree was returning to both of them. There were subtle changes he noticed, nothing too significant, a greater awareness she had of him, like when she would greet him with a drink, give him a bath, initiate the lovemaking. He did not know that much of what motivated this new détente was the guilt consuming her, the guilt she buried until it rose out of her in small acts of generosity. He thought it was a conscious attempt to reengage their marriage, and he did not question it, did not move into it with a lust of his own, but rather simply accepted it as something she needed to do, something that made sense.

For Christmas, Wallace brought Nora a pair of ice skates he had seen in a window in Montpelier, and they were white leather with sharp blades, and when she opened the box he saw her face open in a wide smile. That afternoon they ate roast goose with trimmings and Guy joined them and after, while the sun was settling below the hills, Guy and Wallace shoveled a clearing on the ice of Mirror Lake. Then, while they both watched, Nora took her first tentative steps onto the glassy ice, and with her cheeks flushed from the cold she began to glide, doing something she had not done since she was a child, something that Wallace was glad he had given to her. She skated out to the edge of where they'd shoveled, then put her hands momentarily behind her back and propelled herself to where the two men stood smoking at the lake's edge, watching her. Wallace loved watching her move; she was graceful and light on her feet and, even when she stumbled, she looked good doing it.

She skated until the daylight had faded and later, when she took the skates off, the blisters from the tight leather had already started to form, but she told Wallace it was worth it, that she had forgotten how good it felt to do something simply because it gave you pleasure.

That night he woke in the middle of the night to find her gone, and he figured she was downstairs and he listened but heard no sounds. He managed to fall back asleep anyway, and when he woke next she had still not returned so he climbed out of bed and made his way downstairs. The living room was dark, as was the kitchen; the only light in the house came from the orange coals in the woodstove. Wallace stopped long enough to put another log in the stove, and when he rose he heard the kitchen door opening and he looked up and in the half-light he saw her, wearing a winter coat and boots over her nightdress.

'What are you doing?'

Nora jumped when she heard his voice. 'Jesus, Wallace. You scared me.'

'I woke up and you were gone.'

'I couldn't sleep. I needed some air. I get that way sometimes.'

'It must be ten degrees outside.'

'I know. It's cold, but it helped me. Cleared my head. I'm ready for bed now.'

Wallace nodded. 'Only a few hours left,' he said.

And then the two of them made their way back upstairs, only this time it was Wallace who could not sleep, and while he lay there he remembered that time in the fall when she had left their bed in the middle of the night, and he wondered what kind of woman left a perfectly good bed in a perfectly good farmhouse to wander in the dark. When Wallace finally drifted off, he had vivid dreams, and in them he saw Nora walking in the winter night, and he dreamt that he could see her from the windows of the house but was unable to stop her, that he was somehow frozen where he stood, and while he watched she walked barefoot on the snowy road and then entered the woods, and he stared at the spot where she left the road until her footprints disappeared. He dreamt that he waited in the window, calling out to her, though she did not return. When he woke he confused the dream with the reality, and for a moment he thought that he'd dreamed waking up and finding her gone, but then he realized that this part was real, and then, feeling the length of her leg against his, he was grateful that she had returned.

THE DAY after Christmas, Nora waited all day for a moment when she could get Guy alone, tell him about the night before, warn him about how close they were to getting caught. But that moment never arrived. Wallace and Guy worked together all day, out in the barn, cleaning the stalls, laying new hay and feed for the cows, milking. During dinner that evening Nora looked out the window to the light in the barn, knowing that Guy was there, and she knew she needed to go to him at least one more time, if only to call it off. She had no idea what Wallace would do if he found out, and it worried her.

After dinner while she did the dishes, Wallace smoked in front of the woodstove, and when she finished she joined him and they sat in silence and she worked on finishing a sweater she had been knitting while Wallace sat alone with his thoughts and his whiskey. At one point she looked over at him, and his eyes caught hers and she smiled and he asked her what she was thinking. She told him that she was thinking of summer and her garden.

'Don't wish your life away,' Wallace said.

In truth she was thinking that he did not deserve this, did not deserve her, not the other way around, as Guy had said. Wallace had been nothing but kind to her and together they had built a life and now she was betraying him in the worst way imaginable. And she knew as she thought it that she had to face it eventually, that it would not simply go away, though she did not know how to reconcile the strength of her feelings toward Guy with her need to honor her husband, her marriage. And when she thought about Guy she thought: It can never be anything other than what it is. She knew they had no future, at least not in the conventional sense, and when she thought this she knew she could break it off, but she also knew she would have to be determined, for when she was in his presence it was another matter entirely.

That night she lay next to Wallace and listened to his breathing grow deeper and steadier. The night was dark outside her window and she could not see anything. She stared at the ceiling until she was certain Wallace was asleep, and then, as she had done many nights over the past several months, she quietly got out of the bed and went downstairs, put her boots on and her coat on over her nightdress.

Outside, it had started snowing and it was windy and dark. The snow fell in big flakes as she walked across the pasture toward the barn, the light from the oil lamp in Guy's window diffused and yellow through the snowfall. Nora walked slowly, and the only sound was the wind, blowing the snow up around her, and it was cold and she pulled the coat tight on her neck.

She opened the barn doors slowly and walked in, and then on the ladder Guy was there as he always was, and his hands came down when she hit the third rung and took hers, pulled her up, and once she was up there he brought her close and kissed her, and she kissed him back, falling into him, wanting to talk and tell him what she had decided, but afraid of him, too, not quite sure how he might react.

'We should talk,' she said.

'Not now,' he said, and he led her over to the bed and then onto it, and she felt his hands on her calves, taking off her boots, and then he was on top of her and lifting her up while he removed her coat, and she did not say anything while he lifted her dress over her head and she was naked before him, comfortable that way like she never was with

Wallace; and she did not say anything when his face moved down her body and his mouth was on her nipples, the soft of her belly. Nora wrapped her hands around his arms and tried to lift him up, and he helped her, leaning up and over her, and soon she felt him against her and soon he was inside her and she leaned back and closed her eyes and felt him move within her.

Perhaps it was because she knew it was the last time he would be inside her, or perhaps it was because the night was cold and forbidding and the snow fell hard, but she gave in to him completely, and with her eyes closed her mind roamed the full range of their togetherness, and after a time she felt it coming and then it did, her closing around him like a fist; and as he continued to move she felt it cascading through her, and the sensations were as bright as light, and when he finished and collapsed on top of her, she was exhausted as if after a day of hard work, and she rolled into his naked body, conforming to it, and with her hands she rubbed his body until she could not anymore. Shortly after, she fell asleep.

When she woke she could see the snow falling clearly out the window, and the light was pale enough to make her uncomfortable. Guy was asleep next to her, and she heard his breathing, deep and regular, and she was about to wake him when she heard the distinct sound of the barn door opening, and she knew it was too late, there was nowhere to go, and she lay unable to move as she heard the footsteps downstairs, and then the creak of the ladder, and she wanted to move, to do something, but she could not, so she lay with his arm around her, on his bed, no covers to provide a modicum of modesty for their nakedness.

WALLACE HAD come to suddenly, and with his arm he reached out where Nora should have been and he felt only the cold sheets. He leaned up on his elbows and looked around and he did not see her, though he saw the impression in the bed. Wallace ran his hands through his hair and then he slowly got out of bed, rose to his feet, and outside he could see the steady falling of the snow in the pale early morning light.

Downstairs he checked the woodstove and put another log in, and then he went to the kitchen and looked around for signs that coffee had been made. But it was clear to him that she was not in the house.

From the rack next to the door Wallace took his Carhartt suit and slipped it on over his T-shirt and boxer shorts, and from the floor he picked up his winter boots and slid those on. Outside he stood in front of the house, and through the snowflakes he looked at the lake, the white expanse of it beneath him, and he looked down the length of the road and he did not see Nora. He stood there for a few minutes as he always did in the morning and, though it was an hour away from daybreak, with his seasoned eyes Wallace knew that the snow would stop later, and that the weak winter sun would emerge through the clouds over the lake.

As he turned around and began to walk toward the house, he thought again of his dream, of Nora disappearing into the woods, and he looked over there, at the woods across the road that led to the high pastures, but of course there was no sign of her, and as he rounded the bend of the house that looked out toward the outbuildings and the barn, he saw her footprints in the snow, partially covered.

Wallace stopped for an instant, looking down at the impression of her boots in the snow, and looking up he saw where they zigzagged across the pasture to the barn. He began to walk.

He walked through the pasture, past the sugar shack, the toolshed, among the sleeping Jerseys, the softly falling snow clinging to their brown and white hides. At the barn door he stopped again and listened, and not hearing anything he opened the door and entered the dark barn, his eyes taking a moment to adjust to the change in the light.

Standing on the wooden floor he looked around, let his eyes roam the stalls, the equipment. He smelled the cows and the hay and, underneath it all, the slight odor of manure. But he did not see his wife, and for the first time it occurred to him that she might be upstairs, with Guy, and soon as he thought it he practically dismissed it.

But he did go to the ladder, stepped on the first rung and listened, thought for a moment about calling out to Guy, and upstairs he heard no sound, and he took another step, and then another, and soon his head was through the hole and he could see the legs of the bed and then he pulled himself up and what he saw came to him in broken fragments of images.

He saw her legs, his legs; he saw Guy's face against the pillow, peaceful in sleep; he saw the length of her flesh, his wife; and then above it all he saw her face, staring back at him, the look in her eyes like nothing he had ever seen before, a mix of fear and bewilderment, a look that wondered what next at the same time it suggested it knew.

Wallace stood tall and silent for what seemed like forever but was in reality only a few seconds. One time at night he had looked out the window and seen a Canadian lynx lying on the hood of his pickup truck, and the big cat was clearly that, a big cat; only when Wallace first saw it he thought it was a deer, even though it made no sense; no deer could curl its legs under like that and no deer had that large feline face. But sometimes, when your mind sees things that should not be there, it takes a moment before things come into focus, and when they do the clarity is so sudden, so startling, it practically knocks the wind out of you.

It was then that Wallace found his voice, but it sounded as if it were coming from outside of him, as if it belonged to someone else, and what he said was an articulation of deep pain more than clear words, but it was what set everything in motion, Nora rising and calling to him, reaching for him; Guy waking with a start, trying to stand, getting tangled in the covers and falling to the floor; Wallace fleeing back down to the barn, trying to quiet the pounding noise in his head.

In the barn he stood stock-still, breathing heavily, everything happening in slow motion. First down the ladder was Guy, and Wallace turned and saw him, saw him coming toward him, and he saw him mouthing words but he could not hear them, could not hear anything for the noise that had grown louder within him, and engulfed him; and Wallace reached to his left, and against a stall leaned the shovel, and he took the cool wooden shaft into his hand and as Guy came at him he swung around quickly and brought the head of the shovel into the air, swinging it like a bat, and the first blow caught Guy up on the shoulders and when he screamed Wallace heard it as his own; and then Wallace reared back and swung again and this time he connected the flat iron back of the shovel near Guy's ear, and he crumpled to the ground and Wallace went to hit him again when he saw Nora, coming down the ladder, and it was her voice he finally heard, crystal clear, and it was her tears he saw, down her face, and he let the shovel fall from his hand and he felt it hit his leg before it reached the floor.

Wallace looked down at Guy, and he looked down at Nora, who kneeled next to him, and he watched as Nora took Guy's head into her lap, and he realized that she was naked, and this somehow struck him as odd, especially as Guy's blood was now on the pale skin of her breasts, her stomach, and he moved his eyes to Nora's face and he saw the pain and in that instant Wallace came back to himself, and the noise in his head was gone, and he began to cry himself, tears flowing down his face, and he went to his knees and when he did he knew Guy was dead, that he had killed him, and he looked away as if that might be enough to make it all stop, enough to bring him back.

SOMETIME THAT morning, as Wallace had thought it would, the snow stopped, and the sun emerged from beneath the heavy clouds and the sky was a bright winter blue. In the barn he wrapped Guy's body in some old horse blankets, then took a wagon chain and tied it around those, and then he lifted him up and into a wheelbarrow. He took an ice auger from a hook on the wall and put that into the wheelbarrow, too.

Once outside he began to push the wheelbarrow across the drive that led to the road, and as he did he looked up, and in the kitchen window of his house he saw Nora, her face, and it reminded him of when they were first married and he would see her there, and how that comforted him. He wanted this to comfort him, too, but he knew it could not; he knew that whatever had been left between them was now completely gone, and he was prepared to accept his fate, regardless of what she decided to do.

Wallace walked with the wheelbarrow in front of him down the road, slowly, straining his arms to keep it moving down the slope, and the sun was bright as it played off the snow, off the lake, and as he walked he was conscious of Nora's eyes following him, but he did not look back, instead stayed focused on the task in front of him.

At the lake Wallace left the wheelbarrow at the edge and walked out on the ice, onto the area that he and Guy had shoveled two days previously, and it had been filled in somewhat by the snow from last night but it was still largely clear, and he thought then of Nora on it, pirouetting in small circles, her arms outstretched toward the sky, the look of bliss on her face.

Wallace walked out to the edge of where they had shoveled, scouting it, and when he was happy it was as he thought, deep enough at that point, he returned to the ice. As he had done since he was a boy, Wallace knelt and using the auger began slowly to cut a hole in the ice. At this time of year the ice was at least eight inches thick, and grooved, and Wallace worked hard to cut the hole, first getting the drill bit in there, then working it slowly around. When one hole was cut, he cut another next to it, and then another across from it, creating a square of holes with ice in the middle. At one point he stopped to wipe the sweat that had beaded up on his forehead, and in that moment he had a memory of cutting through the ice with his father, when he was a child, and it was not often that he thought back that far, and he remembered thinking with the mind of a child that it did not make sense to be able to do this, to slice through the ice and have water underneath and fish to catch. At that time he thought if the surface was ice then the whole thing should be too, and he remembered asking his father that question, and he remembered the deep-bellied laugh his father gave in reply.

When the four holes were cut to his satisfaction, he pushed down on the center with his boot and it gave, breaking into different pieces as chunks of ice bobbed now on the surface of the black water. Wallace then walked to the shore, where he retrieved the wheelbarrow, brought it onto the ice, and then, straining, he lifted Guy out of it, placed him on the ice next to the hole, checked the chain to see that it was tight, checked the blankets to see that they were in place. With his boots and his hands he pushed Guy toward the hole, and when he reached it he pushed harder, so that the whole mass fell into the black water at once, bobbing slightly up for a second before slipping quickly down into the depths, disappearing below the surface.

Later, Wallace took Guy's things out of the room upstairs, his clothes, his bedding, anything and everything that was his, and out in front of the barn in the snow he built a fire with kindling, and then piled all of the stuff on top of it, and he stood there smoking and watched it burn, the smoke rising up and into the clear blue sky, floating over the house in black wisps toward Mirror Lake. And while he did, Wallace wondered if Nora was watching it too, wondered what she thought, and in that moment he decided he was too far gone to care anyway.

THAT NIGHT Wallace did not eat, and he did not see Nora. He went inside briefly to get some blankets and a bottle of whiskey, and then he sat on the porch and drank and looked at the lake, watched the sky darken until it was pitch black and star-filled. The night grew cold, but still he did not care; he brought the blankets up around him and he continued to sip the whiskey until it was gone, rolling his cigarettes as fast as they were smoked. He watched the lake in the dark, and he thought that he could see the hole he had cut, the hole he had pushed Guy into, never to return. But he knew that that was in his mind, for his eyes were not that good to pick it up from here, and he knew that by the morning the ice would have grown back, sealed it up, as if it had never happened.

In the morning he rose and did the milking as usual, and his body ached from the night in the chair and his head pounded from the booze but he kept on, doing the work of the farm, and at lunch he saw Nora in the kitchen and he knew that she was doing the same thing. That night they ate dinner together in silence, and for the next year they moved around each other like ghosts. Wallace moved into a room downstairs, and when they talked it was about necessary things, and they never made love or acted at all like husband and wife, which Wallace tolerated because he was grateful simply to have her in the house.

Then one late spring day he looked up from where he was tilling the field and he saw her, standing on the steps that led down from the kitchen, and she had in her hand a suitcase and another one behind her and he knew that this was the end.

Wallace went to her and he did not question anything, he simply asked her where she needed to go and she said the train, and so he helped her with her bags and then drove her to St J. and the station. At the station it was the same as it was at the house, and he unloaded her bags and there were no good-byes, and he realized as he watched the train pull away that they had said their good-byes already, said them on a winter day when the snowfall quickly turned to sun, on a winter day when Wallace killed a man with a shovel and buried him in the only lake he had ever known.

16

We sat in silence for what seemed like forever. Below us the lake was a crystal blue, and the sun was a bright yellow ball above the hills beyond it. I could hardly look at Wallace, and he could hardly look at me, and as the telling went on his voice had dropped to almost a whisper, and by the time he told me he had killed Guy I had to strain to pick out his words, which I would have had to do anyway, for I had never known anyone before who had killed a man, though in that moment when he told it to me I thought that we were all capable of it given the right circumstances; though later I wondered if that was really true, and I decided that I hoped I would never find out for certain.

When I finally spoke, my question was simple. 'Did you ever see Nora again?'

'No,' he said. 'Never.'

I nodded. I thought about what else to ask, and I realized that I knew everything, that there was nothing else for me to say to Wallace, and so I stood and I went to him and I put my hand on his shoulder and he did not look up but he did take his own hand and place it on mine.

A week later I got the call I suppose I had been expecting all along. Someone driving past his house had seen Wallace lying on the ground next to the lake, and they were not going to stop when they thought that perhaps they should, and sure enough when they reached him he was dead. Linger was the one who called me, as he seemed to be the conduit for all information in the town, and I did not cry or break down when I heard: I suppose I thought that it was his time, that he had finished the story he needed to tell and he could now move on.

As it turned out, later in that same day I received a call from a lawyer in St J. who informed me that I was the sole beneficiary of Wallace's will, which meant that I now owned his house and the land and the lake itself, and that there was a safe-deposit box full of money that was mine, too.

The first thing I did was talk to Kate about a funeral and, since there were no instructions, we bought a simple coffin from the funeral home where he was removed to, and we decided that we would bury him on his land, and I made the decision to have him buried near the apple tree on the top of the hill, close to the son they almost had, and out of direct view of the lake itself.

The next thing I did was reprise my trip to Jay, New York,

setting out early the next morning, crossing Lake Champlain in brilliant sunshine, the bluish mountains rising out of the earth along its shore, driving through the deep green Adirondacks, following the pebbly-bottomed Ausable River as it wove through the tree-filled hillsides. I found my way to Nora's house by memory, and when I got there she was sitting on the porch, as if she had been expecting me.

She did not budge when I got out of the car, and though it was late May and the day was warm, she wore a long skirt and a cardigan sweater pulled tight around her small frame. Her gray hair was down and longer than I remembered, almost down to her waist.

'He's dead, isn't he?' she said, when I reached the porch.

I sat down in a wooden chair next to her. I could see all the mountains from here, and in the pastures in front of us a stiff breeze bent the tall green grass back.

'Yes,' I said. 'He is.'

Nora nodded at me. 'When?'

'Two days ago.'

'Did you find him?'

'No. It was a heart attack. Down by the lake.'

She nodded her head. I saw that her hands were gripping the arms of the rocking chair tight, and I could see her pronounced veins, rising up like mountain ridges underneath her skin. She did not say anything else. I said, 'We are burying him tomorrow, on the land. I thought you might want to be there. I can drive you.'

'It was nice of you to come.'

'He would have wanted you there.'

Nora looked away from me, toward the east and the mountains, toward Vermont, toward Eden. 'You can't go back.'

The following morning we buried Wallace without Nora, buried him on the hilly land across the road from his house. It was Kate and I, and Linger, and two guys from the funeral home who lowered the casket into the ground and then waited while I said a few words, something I had not fully thought about doing before I did it, though I suppose I knew it needed to be done. I did not talk about Nora, or about Guy, or about anything like that. Instead I talked about the times he made me dinner, the times he listened to me talk, that first time when he pulled my Jeep out of the ravine, took me to his house, fed me venison. I told about how much pride he took in the farm, how he loved the land like a child. And then I said the one thing I knew beyond a shadow of a doubt about this complex man I had come to know: He was my friend.

When I finished, the three of us threw dirt on the coffin, and then Linger handed me a cigarette, and Kate took one, too, and the three of us smoked over Wallace's open grave, and it was another beautiful day in a string of beautiful days, a pale blue cloudless sky, a soft breeze, the golden green of spring all around us.

After, we drove to the bar, and Linger made us roast beef sandwiches, and Kate and I drank beer out of the tap while Linger drank Cokes. We tried our best to make it feel like a funeral, and I told stories about Wallace, every story I knew, that is, except the one that defined his life.

In the days that followed I put Wallace's house and farm on the market, and it sold for more than I asked for, and it sold quickly, to a couple in their thirties from Burlington, a software engineer and his wife and their baby boy and, for the first time in Eden's history, Mirror Lake was no longer Fiske land.

As for me, the sale made me not rich but comfortable, and the first thing I did was resign my job at the post office, while I tried to figure out what to do next. I decided against doing anything quickly and instead decided I would enjoy the summer in Eden, and I would enjoy Kate, and I would try not to take things too seriously. It was the best plan I'd had in a while.

ONE EVENING that summer Kate and I hiked through the woods to our Mirror Lake, which I had seen only in winter, and in the darkness, and when we arrived the sun was down but there was still plenty of light in the sky, and we laid out a blanket on its shore and watched the dragonflies skim across the surface, listened to the birds in the trees, and looked around at the ridges that framed the small, perfect lake.

We brought with us a cooler, and we drank chilled champagne out of paper cups, and ate bread with sausage and cheese, but mostly we just sat there in silence and looked at the lake and leaned against each other. It was a remarkable night, clear and comfortable, and when it grew dark we could still see fine but Kate pulled a votive candle out of her bag and lit it, which I objected to, since I thought it would attract insects.

'Shush,' she said, and I could see why she liked it for, though it gave off little light, it still lit up the world around us, and its flame was visible in the water in front of us, larger than it actually was, stretching long and thin away from us.

As we sat there, Kate reached into her bag and brought something else out, and this time she held it behind her back.

'I have something for you,' she said.

'What?'

'It's a surprise.'

'Come on, Kate,' I said. 'I hate surprises.'

She handed it to me then, and it was a small box, and I said, 'What is it?'

'Open it,' she said, and I did, and it was a ring, and I looked at her and she had a wicked smile on her face, and at that moment she did one of those gestures I love, where she takes her hand and pulls the hair away from her face, tucks it behind her ears. It's a gesture that women the world over do, but one that she seems somehow to make particular to her.

'What is this?' I said.

Kate took my hand then. 'It's pretty obvious, Nathan,' she said. 'I want you to marry me.'

I laughed. 'Are you asking me or telling me?'

'I'm asking,' she said.

I looked at her and smiled. 'Well, fuck you, then,' I said, and she pushed me, and I pushed her back, and then she smacked me on the side of the head and I reached out and did the same. Then she said, 'Okay, enough,' and I stopped and she stopped and then we kissed, then we held each other and she pulled away from me.

'Well?' she said.

'Well what?'

'Are you going to marry me, asshole?'

'That's nice, Kate,' I said. 'Probably the first time those words have ever been put together. But I shouldn't even have to say the answer. 'Cause you know what it is.'

'You have to say it, Nathan. Those are the rules.'

And so I said it, took the plunge. I said, 'Yes.' 'Yes' is what I said, and in that moment a fish broke the surface of the lake in front of us with a loud plop, shattering the silence on Mirror Lake, our Mirror Lake.

WE SOMETIMES spend our lives running from things, and the day I married Kate was, I think, the day I effectively stopped running. She wore a white dress and I wore my suit and it was as simple as a wedding can be, ten minutes in the town clerk's office with Linger as our witness. But as simple as that wedding was, I can tell you that on that day there was no more beautiful woman in the world than Kate Linger, a bartender's daughter from tiny Eden, Vermont. When we said those simple words that people say the world over, I could not stop looking at her, at her eyes, her face, and I knew that both our lives had conspired to bring us to this one point, this place, this room, this state, and that from now on when I needed a marker to lean on, it was this I would look to as the defining moment for the next chapter of my life.

After, the three of us drove out to Mirror Lake on my request. When we arrived, I went around to Kate's door, and I pulled her out and lifted her in my arms and, while she shrieked for me to put her down, I walked to the lake's shore and dropped her in her white dress into the water, watched her come up sputtering, her hair matted down against her beautiful face, Linger chuckling behind me as Kate cursed at me, but I did not care because I could not be more in love with anyone than I was with her at that moment. Later, we retired to the bar and Linger poured us drinks and it was like Wallace's funeral except that there were other people in the bar and they raised their glasses to us. As we drank, Kate glared at me in her wet dress, but I knew she was not really mad; sometimes you have to do the things that tie you to the past, and this was one of them.

Three days later, as was our pact, we left Eden and moved back to Boston. With the money I had from the sale of Wallace's house, I intended to buy us a place to live and start anew. Before I went, though, I had one more thing I needed to do.

And so on a warm summer day, not unlike the one I found when I first arrived in Eden, I drove out to Wallace's place, out to Mirror Lake, one last time. As I drove I remembered Nora's words, that you can't go back. I was determined, at least in this small way, to show that you could.

The new family, people named Lehmann, the Burlington software engineer and his wife and infant boy, had already moved in, and when I pulled in the driveway the husband was outside painting the side of the house. I was pleased to see it would still be white.

They were surprised to see me, and offered me iced tea, which I accepted and, with this couple and their baby in a chair, I sat on the porch that Wallace and I had sat on so many times, talking late into the night, drinking and smoking, looking at the clear water below us. They told me their plans for the house, where the swing set would go, how they intended to plant an apple orchard where the barn stands, tearing it down because it would not be safe when the child grew older.

While they talked, I did my best to pretend to listen, though I heard little of what they said. Instead, my thoughts were on Wallace, on Nora, and yes, on Guy, and I wondered not only where love can go wrong but where it can go right, and while the story – the lives – they lived was fundamentally tragic, in between there were moments of great beauty, moments of true passion, and moments of happiness that cannot be discounted despite everything else that went on.

When I finally left, I stopped for a moment by the lake's shore, and I looked out to where on a Christmas Day years ago Nora had skated on the ice. The sun was out and there was no wind. The lake was as still as glass. And as I looked at the water I became aware of the vast unknown history of all things, the water and the land and the mountains, the ineffable sweep of time. And what I felt was awe and wonder and greatness. I knew then that all we are given in this world are choices, choices about how we love and live, and choices about what we leave behind. And the truth is, in the end, all we are, all we can ever be, are stories, stories that must be told, as I have told this one. Wallace believed this and now I do as well, and when you believe it fully you can no longer be afraid and you can no longer be alone.

I left Vermont, and I left Mirror Lake, but they have never left me. Today when Kate comes in the door with her arms full of groceries, her face flush with the glow of the city, I will feel a quickening in my heart, and I will go to her, and I will hold her, and I will feel the swelling of her belly against mine.

And in time we will grow old.